Note to readers:

I'm not sharing this script because it's perfect or because I'm holding it up as a stellar piece of screenwriting. My own skills and technique improved in the years after this script was written, and there are plenty of produced scripts around that set the bar higher than most of us will ever reach.

I'm offering this script to those people who want to see what a Nicholl Fellowship*-winning script in 2001 looked like (and there are many of you who do) and for those who want to compare it to the novel that inspired it, *La Desperada*.

I have written a book for others like me who dreamed of seeing their novels on the silver screen, *Adapting Your Novel Into an Award-Winning Script (And Why You Don't Want To, A Cautionary Tale)* which heavily references this script and the source novel. So for those who want to really dig in and compare the two, here is the script you've been asking for to go with the novel, which has been available for several years.

The formatting in this script simulates an industry script, but the margins and layout are not exactly the same, nor do screenwriters use double-sided pages. These choices were made to keep the production costs as low as possible.

I wish you luck and joy in all your writing dreams and endeavors, whether they are about publication or production. Write with energy, live with joy, and at the end of the day, you'll have accomplished far more than the people who never tried.

~ *Pooks*

* *The Academy of Motion Picture Arts and Science's Don and Gee Nicholl Fellowships in Screenwriting is an international screenwriting competition established to identify and encourage talented new screenwriters. Up to five $35,000 Fellowships are awarded annually. There were 5,489 entries the year I won my Fellowship, and 4,250 entries the previous year, when I was a Finalist. I am the only screenwriter in the history of the competition who achieved Finalist status with two different scripts.*

OTHER BOOKS BY PATRICIA BURROUGHS

REDEMPTION

Inspired by the Novel

La Desperada

(previously published as *What Wild Ecstasy*)

both by

Patricia Burroughs

 Book View Café

Book View Café
P.O. Box 1624
Cedar Crest, NM 87008-1624
http://bookviewcafe.com/

In 2001 Patricia Burroughs was awarded a prestigious "Don and Gee Nicholl Fellowship in Screenwriting" by the Academy of Motion Picture Arts and Sciences in Los Angeles. The script, "Redemption," is an adaptation of her first published novel, *La Desperada*, previously titled *What Wild Ecstasy*.

By making this script available as a supplement to her book, *Adapting Your Novel Into an Award-Winning Script (And Why You Don't Want To, A Cautionary Tale)* she allows its use for educational purposes only. No other rights are granted with the purchase of this script.

Her heartfelt gratitude goes to Mrs. Gee Nicholl, who endowed the Don and Gee Nicholl Fellowships, and to all those at the Academy who work diligently to continue its amazing work, in particular, Mr. Greg Beal, its director for almost twenty-five years.

Publisher's Note: This is a work of fiction. Names, characters, places, and incidents are a product of the author's imagination. Locales and public names are sometimes used for atmospheric purposes. Any resemblance to actual people, living or dead, or to businesses, companies, events, institutions, or locales is completely coincidental.

Redemption ~ An Award-Winning Screenplay/ Patricia Burroughs. -- 1st ed.
ISBN 978 1 61138 314 0

FADE IN:

EXT. BOONE CREEK, MISSOURI - NIGHT

A foggy clearing in the trees. A ghostly fire CRACKLES and blazes against the night sky - a cabin ablaze.

Maybe, just maybe, SCREAMS can be heard from inside.

Maybe, just maybe, a baby CRYING.

And as the roof collapses and sparks fly into the foggy heavens a seventeen-year-old boy throws back his head and screams in agony--

                    JOHN WESLEY BRIDGES (O.S.)
          Murderers!

EXT. WEST TEXAS - NIGHT

BOONE COULTER - a tortured man tired of living but too skilled a fighter to die - jerks up from his bedroll, shaking, sweating.

He clutches his stomach and rolls to his side. He clenches his eyes closed, and maybe, just maybe, we hear the faint CRACKLING of fire and SCREAMS.

INT. DORALEE'S ROOM - NIGHT

A young whore and a man asleep.

The man, SHERIFF CLAYTON DOUGHERTY, bolts upright. He's a large, handsome man beginning to deteriorate from liquor and hard living.

Dougherty stares into the night.

And faintly ... CRACKLE. ... SCREAM.

EXT. WEST TEXAS - DAWN

Sunrise.

INT. ELIZABETH'S BEDROOM - DAY

ELIZABETH DOUGHERTY, a Victorian woman wearing a high-necked nightgown tosses restlessly in bed. The sheets twist around her and her long blond hair tangles around her face and shoulders.

A rooster CROWS.

Elizabeth sits at the edge of the bed, chafing her arms.

A dog BARKS outside.

She rummages through her dressing table drawer and finds a small, brown glass bottle. She opens it, attempts with shaking hands to pour it into a glass. The bottle is empty. Desperately, she licks the rim.

The bottle falls to the tabletop. Trembling, she gropes through the drawer. Finally, she braces herself against the table and takes a deep, shuddering breath.

She pulls a photograph from the drawer, a picture of a handsome man. She touches his face.

The dog outside BARKS wildly, then YELPS in pain.

She panics, casts a desperate glance out the window.

The yelp fades into a pitiful HOWL then a WHIMPER.

Frantic, she thrusts the photograph and the bottle into the drawer and slams it shut.

She hovers by the door, listening.

Silence.

She opens the door to find an empty hallway.

EXT. REDEMPTION, TEXAS - STREET - DAY

A dusty town. No building is over a few years old but there's little paint or effort to maintain civic pride.

DEPUTY MICAH BRIDGES, eighteen years old and all angles and elbows, rides up, leading a small pack horse with Boone Coulter (the sick guy on the bedroll) slung across its back. His wrists and ankles are bound; his head hangs limply.

A SIX-YEAR-OLD BOY runs into the road ahead of him and points.

                         BOY
          Ma! Micah killed somebody!

Coulter moves. The boy yelps. His MOTHER grabs him.

TWO IDLERS watch from the doorway of the saloon.

                        IDLER 1
          Can't you leave a poor fella alone, let him sleep
          off his drunk in private?

Micah dismounts, agitated.

                              MICAH
          Sheriff upstairs?

                              IDLER 2
          Can't handle a drunk by yerself?

                              IDLER 1
          Hell, no. If the feller weren't drunk and disabled,
          Micah couldn't catch him by hisself.

INT. DORALEE'S ROOM - NIGHT

The whore and the man - still asleep.

The whore, DORALEE - blond, eighteen, dirty - sits up in bed when
she hears HOOFBEATS below. She flips back the curtain and peers
down on the street.

Dougherty grabs her arm.

                              DOUGHERTY
          What's going on?

                              DORALEE
          Micah brung somebody in.

                              DOUGHERTY
          What the hell ...

He raises up to look out the window.

                              DOUGHERTY
          Who the hell'd he find to arrest?

EXT. REDEMPTION, TEXAS STREET - DAY

Micah darts anxious glances at Coulter as he ties the horses up at
the jail across from the saloon.

The men in the saloon doorway fall aside as Dougherty emerges,
dressed but disheveled.

                              MICAH
                         (grinning)
          I caught me an outlaw.

                              DOUGHERTY
          Who is it?

Dougherty grabs a fistful of Coulter's hair and yanks his head up
to look.

                              MICAH
          Boone Coulter!

Dougherty steps back, stunned.

Coulter looks like hell, but is conscious.

                              IDLER 2
          Sheeyit! Micah, you couldn't catch Boone Coulter if
          he rode up and turned hisself in.

                              IDLER 1
          I reckon Micah's the one's drunk.

More men come pouring out of the saloon, followed by Doralee,
buttoning her bodice.

Dougherty grabs Coulter and drags him off the horse.

Coulter lands on the ground in a heap, but manages to pull to a
sitting position, his expression sending lethal messages he's
obviously unable to carry through. The crowd from the saloon
presses forward.

                              MALE VOICE
          What makes you so sure he's Coulter?

                              MICAH
          His horse.

He yanks his hat off his head and shows an ugly gash.

                              MICAH
          See what that wildass horse of his did to me?

They're impressed. And beginning to take him a little seriously -
especially Doralee - but not Dougherty, who can't take his eyes
off Coulter, nor Coulter him.

Something's going on here, something nobody else notices.

Doralee dabs a bandanna at the oozing gash on Micah's head. He
tries to ignore her.

                              DORALEE
          Somebody needs to stitch that up.

                              MICAH
          It was Coulter's horse, I tell you - black, with
          scars all over its haunches. I tried to bring it
          in, too, but after it did this to me, it took off
          like wild fire.

Everybody drops back, a little concerned. Even bound, Coulter strikes fear in them.

                    IDLER 2
          How the hell did you catch him?

                    MICAH
          I found him hunkered over a rock, takin' a shit -
          sick as a dog.

                    NEW MALE VOICE:
          Whattid he do when he seed ya'?

Micah thinks, scratches his nose, shrugs.

                    MICAH
          He just shat.

The crowd laughs. Micah spins and faces Dougherty.

                    MICAH
          Somebody's gotta wire Fort Davis, Sheriff. Let 'em
          know I got Coulter, so's I can get my reward.

At the word "reward," Doralee perks up.

                    DOUGHERTY
          First you've gotta get him behind bars, Micah.

Micah cuts the ropes at Coulter's ankles, then pulls his gun and holds the barrel against Coulter's neck.

                    MICAH
          Listen here, mister. Get up nice and easy, no funny
          business.

Coulter staggers to his feet and glares not at Micah, but straight into Dougherty's insolent gaze.

INT. JAIL - DAY

The cell door CLANGS shut.

Coulter slumps against the wall at the front of the cell, his hands still bound.

                    DOUGHERTY (SOFTLY)
          Well, well, John Wesley. I always wondered what
          happened to you.

Coulter throws his head back at that name.

                              MICAH
        Who's John Wesley?

Dougherty whirls to find Micah right behind him. He jerks his head
toward the front door.

                            DOUGHERTY
        Get out of here. Get something to eat.

Micah starts to leave.

                            DOUGHERTY
        I'm proud of you, boy. You've done a man's work
        today.

                              MICAH
        Thank you, Sheriff.

He smiles shyly and leaves.

Dougherty turns back to the cell. Coulter can barely force the
words out, but his venom gives them strength -

                            COULTER
        John Wesley Bridges died that night at Boone Creek.
        You'd best remember that.

EXT. STREET IN FRONT OF HOTEL - DAY

A loud CLOP-CLOPPING announces the approach of a buggy.

EXT. GENERAL STORE - DAY

The buggy is parallel to the plank sidewalk. Elizabeth climbs down
from the buggy.

INT. GENERAL STORE - DAY

Elizabeth stands at the counter, dabbing her face with her
handkerchief. MRS. JACKSON is assisting her.

                          MRS. JACKSON
        About the -
                    (lowers voice)
        Female remedy, Miz Dougherty. We're out of Dr.
        Kilmer's Female Tonic. If it comes in on next
        week's stage...

                          ELIZABETH
        Next week? I can't wait that long.

Mrs. Jackson's voice drops lower, more sympathetic.

                         MRS. JACKSON
          I have something stronger. Some laudanum?

She offers a small vial for Elizabeth's approval.

                         MRS. JACKSON
          Mind you, the opium's stronger than what you're
          used to. This isn't an elixir. You only need five
          drops in a cup of water, if that.

                         ELIZABETH
          I .. I think I'll keep it with me.

Elizabeth wraps the bottle in her handkerchief and tucks it into
her drawstring purse. Mrs. Jackson gathers her purchases - French
soaps and embroidery thread - and wraps them in brown paper.

                         MRS. JACKSON
          Isn't that something about Micah? Of all people -
          bringing in that killer.

                         ELIZABETH
          What?

                         MRS. JACKSON
          Hard to believe isn't it?

                         ELIZABETH
          Is Micah all right?

The BELL JANGLES, announcing a customer. Mrs. Jackson huffs up as
DORALEE enters and surveys the interior of the store with a sneer.
She saunters to the counter.

                         DORALEE
          I hope I'm not interruptin' anything.

                         MRS. JACKSON
          You know better than to come in here with decent
          folks, Doralee. Go on, git out of ...

                         ELIZABETH
          No.

Doralee and Mrs. Jackson both turn to stare at Elizabeth.
Elizabeth looks away, embarrassed.

                         ELIZABETH
          Please. Take care of your customer.

                         MRS. JACKSON
          I'll only be a minute, Miz Dougherty.

Scowling at Doralee, she bustles through the storeroom door.

Elizabeth studies Doralee.

Doralee fixes her kohl-lined eyes on Elizabeth, and smirks.

> DORALEE
> Well, now. I sure have heard a lot about you. All
> true, too, I'll wager.

Doralee begins to laugh.

> DORALEE
> You poor thing.

> ELIZABETH
> I - I beg your pardon?

> DORALEE
> You know exactly what I'm sayin. You wanta please a
> man, maybe you need to try what I'm tryin, and it
> sure ain't soap. You gotta be what a man wants you
> to be, and that ain't squeaky clean and uppity.

Elizabeth slowly arches her eyebrows.

> ELIZABETH
> Then it's no wonder you please him so well.

> DORALEE
> I only have to please him a few hours at a time,
> and only until I find a way out of this hell hole.
> Please him or not, you're stuck with him for the
> rest of your days.

They exchange a long look.

Mrs. Jackson comes out from the storeroom with a brown paper-
wrapped package.

> MRS. JACKSON
> I found your henna, and your other things, Doralee.
> Now get out of here.

Doralee begins to retrieve a few coins from her pocketbook. She
spills the contents on the floor.

> DORALEE
> Damnation!

Elizabeth hesitates, but after a moment, she drops to the floor
with Doralee. Flustered, Doralee tries to scoop up her

belongings.

                    ELIZABETH
          You've missed some.

Doralee looks suspicious, but Elizabeth seems sincere as she
presses the last coin into Doralee's palm.

Elizabeth clutches her own pocketbook desperately to her body as
she stands. She sways, grabs the counter.

                    MRS. JACKSON
          Are you all right, ma'am?

                    ELIZABETH
          I really must go.

She is halfway to the door when Ms. Jackson catches up, gives her
the parcel.

                    MRS. JACKSON
          Don't forget your toiletries. I'll put them all on
          the sheriff's bill.

                    ELIZABETH
          Yes. Please. Thank you.

She stops, looking back at Doralee who still clutches her handful
of change.

                    ELIZABETH
          Put hers on his bill, too. It's his money any way
          you look at it.

The door slams behind her as Mrs. Jackson gasps.

EXT. GENERAL STORE - DAY

Elizabeth climbs into the buggy, trembling. She pulls away from
the sidewalk, urging the horse faster.

Doralee bursts out of the store. Mrs. Jackson follows.

                    DORALEE
          I don't take charity offa nobody! You hear me?
          Nobody!

She hurls her package. It hits the back of Elizabeth's buggy and
explodes.

French soaps and embroidery threads scatter in the dirt.

Doralee kicks more dirt over them, and bursts out laughing.

> DORALEE
> Well, Miz Jackson, you'd better put my shit on the
> sheriff's bill after all, cause I sure as hell
> don't give to charity, either!

But she picks up one of the soaps, sniffs it, and shoves it in her blouse. She flounces off.

EXT. ROAD OUTSIDE OF TOWN - DAY

Sweating, trembling, Elizabeth reins in the horses.

She fumbles with her purse until she finds the opium, then taps two drops into her mouth.

She grips the buggy seat and shudders.

INT. JAIL - NIGHT

Coulter slumps against the wall, his eyes closed.

> DOUGHERTY
> I don't know what the hell I'm gonna do with you.

Dougherty sweeps his hand across the desk and sends everything flying.

At that, Coulter opens his eyes and looks up at him. Coulter takes a pained breath. Each word is an effort.

> COULTER
> I could have killed you years ago.

> DOUGHERTY
> Brave words from behind bars.

Coulter raises his bound hands and tries to flex them. When he looks back at Dougherty, his gaze is steady.

> COULTER
> Brave enough to give everybody who comes after me a
> fair fight, Dougherty. You wanta kill me - let me
> out, say I tried to escape ... or are you afraid I
> will?

Dougherty walks slowly, warily to his desk and sinks into the chair. He steeples his fingers over the knife on the desk, hunches forward.

                    DOUGHERTY
        I don't dare let you go to trial, cause ... well,
        we both know why, don't we, John Wesley?

Coulter stiffens.

                    DOUGHERTY
        Don't like me to use that name, do you? Wouldn't
        your daddy love thumping his Bible over your sins?
        My, my, how you've changed.

                    COULTER
        More than you think, Dougherty ... or you'd be dead
        already.

Coulter stares up at Dougherty.

                    COULTER
        Time finished what you started. Susannah's dead.

Dougherty picks up his knife, runs his thumb lovingly down the
edge.

                    DOUGHERTY
        So are you. As soon as I figure out how to do it.

Their eyes meet in a silent duel. Coulter takes in a shuddering
breath. His lips curl with the hint of a sneer and quietly, his
voice the rustle of a rattlesnake ....

                    COULTER
        Why don't you just burn down the jail... with me in
        it?
                    (beat)
        We both know you're good at that.

Dougherty flings his knife on the desk and hurtles across the
jail. He unlocks the cell door and hauls Coulter to his feet.

                    DOUGHERTY
        I'm pretty damned good at this, too, you son-of-a-
        bitch.

He lets loose with his fist - Coulter's head pops back. Dougherty
steps back as Coulter collapses on the floor.

Sunlight floods the room as the jail door opens. Micah hastily
shuts the door behind him.

                    MICAH
        What's happenin', sheriff?

Dougherty backs out of the cell and SLAMS the cell door shut, fighting for control. Scowling, he averts his eyes from Micah.

> DOUGHERTY
> Son-of-a-bitch insulted me.

Micah stands at the cell, peering in worriedly at Coulter's limp body. Dougherty opens the jail door and leans against the jamb, heaving in great gulps of air.

> DOUGHERTY
> I don't want anybody in here.
> Nobody talks to him, understand?

> MICAH
> Yessir.

Dougherty slams out of the jail.

Micah closes the door and locks it. He prods Coulter through the bars with the toe of his boot.

> MICAH
> You okay in there, mister?

Coulter groans. Micah takes his knife and, since the outlaw's hands are near the bars, slices the rope.

Satisfied, Micah fetches a mug of coffee from the stove and sinks into Dougherty's chair, propping his boots on the desk.

> MICAH
> Must have been some derned insult.

INT. ELIZABETH'S BEDROOM - NIGHT

Elizabeth taps three drops of opium into a small glass of water.

She stands at the window, sipping, and stares into the night, her hair loose and tangled. She opens a button at her neck, pulls a gold cross from within her nightgown, slides it back and forth, back and forth. A tear rolls down her cheek.

INT. SALOON - NIGHT

Dougherty pushes through the doors. SEVERAL MEN are at the makeshift bar, a long varnished plank stretched over several whiskey barrels. The BARTENDER sees Dougherty and hurriedly signals through a torn curtain.

Dougherty rounds the bar to wait by the curtain. Doralee emerges. Dougherty grabs her arm and yanks her to him.

> DORALEE
>> Well, hello, sugar.

He shoves her back through the curtain.

INT. SALOON STAIRCASE - CONTINUOUS

Dougherty pushes Doralee up the narrow staircase. At the top, three crude doors are closed. He shoulders open the last one.

INT. DORALEE'S ROOM - CONTINUOUS

Dougherty thrusts Doralee inside, slams the door. She falls back on her elbows on the bed, and grins.

> DORALEE
>> I figgered you'd be by to see me.

He bends over her and closes his hand around her throat. A thrill of nervousness flickers across her face. She closes her hand lightly over his and moves it to her breast.

> DORALEE
>> I know just what you need.

He pulls his hand away.

> DOUGHERTY
>> What the hell happened at Jackson's Store?

She slinks to her feet and sneers.

> DORALEE
>> Don't blame it on me - it was that bitch wife of
>> yours who -

> DOUGHERTY
>> You talked to my wife? You dared approach my wife
>> in public?

He raises his hand to strike her.

The sound of LOUD LAUGHTER comes from downstairs. Dougherty looks from Doralee to the door.

He lowers his hand. The expression in his eyes is cold, deadly. Doralee oozes up to him, kisses his chin. Strokes the hair away from his eyes. He catches her hands.

> DOUGHERTY
>> It better not happen again, understand? You don't
>> talk to my wife again. Ever.

Her face twists and she jerks away from him.

He pulls two silver dollars out of his pocket and tucks them into her bodice - one over each nipple. She smiles.

                    DOUGHERTY
          If you want more, make me happy.

He jerks her face up to his as he gropes her body with his other hand. She whimpers into his mouth, then bites his lower lip, drawing blood.

                    DORALEE
          You son-of-a-bitch - I always make you happy.

Their mouths fuse in a hot kiss.

INT. ELIZABETH'S BEDROOM - NIGHT

Elizabeth sits at her dressing table, brushing her hair. She's in a dressing gown. Her brush strokes are long, languid, drugged. Before her are the empty water glass and the photo.

A door SLAMS downstairs. As FOOTSTEPS climb the stairs, she stumbles to close her bedroom door - Dougherty's hand stops the door from closing. He shoves the door open. She falls back. He looms over her, leans against the doorjamb.

                    DOUGHERTY
          Don't know why you bother to lock the door. You
          could prance nekkid down the hall, and I wouldn't
          come after you.

                    ELIZABETH
          You've been drinking.

                    DOUGHERTY
          And why the hell not? I'm married to a dried up
          spinster who --

She slaps him - hard - jerks her hand away, horrified. She backs up a step.

                    ELIZABETH
          I'm sorry. I shouldn't have -
                    (deep breath)
          Clayton, I've decided to leave you.

His expression turns to stone.

                    ELIZABETH
          I refuse to live this way any more.

                    DOUGHERTY
          What do you mean - this way? I built you this
          goddamn house!

She paces away from him nervously.

                    ELIZABETH
          It's not the house - it's not even your
          philandering, it's, it's -

She whirls to face him, pleading.

                    ELIZABETH
          It's this life! I can't survive in this place!

                    DOUGHERTY
          You think I'm going to let you leave? After I took
          pity on you, married you, set you up in the finest
          house anybody in these parts has ever seen - and
          you think I'm going to let you leave?

                    ELIZABETH
          For God's sake, why do you care?

He grabs her face with both hands and squeezes, shoves her against
the wall.

                    DOUGHERTY
          How do you think you'll leave? You think you can
          just step on that mail stage to Marfa and I won't
          haul you back off? You think there's a lawman in
          Texas who won't send you back to me?

She struggles. He grabs her necklace and pulls it tighter,
tighter, until it snaps. The cross flies loose and hits the
floor.

                    ELIZABETH
                    (choking)
          Micah gave that to me!

                    DOUGHERTY
                    (sneering)
          Just like Micah to give a whore's necklace to a - a
          dried up spinster bitch who cries over a dead man
          because you don't know what to do with a live one.

Then, drawing from deep inside -

                    ELIZABETH
          A dead man - your brother - who could turn a dried-
          up spinster into a woman on fire.

He explodes. Grabs a fistful of her hair and slams her head against the wall. She falls to the floor. Scrambles to the door.

He grabs the back of her dressing gown - the fabric sash rips loose - he yanks her to her feet - wraps the sash around her neck - pulls tighter - tighter --

Choking, gasping, she claws at his face, beats at his shoulders with her fists - as a last, desperate effort gropes wildly until her left hand grabs an oil lamp on the dressing table -

She smashes it against the side of his head.

Dougherty falls back, howling with pain, as kerosene runs down his face, burning into the jagged cuts.

Elizabeth clutches her throat, coughing, crying, as she scrambles to the door.

Dougherty roars and takes after her.

INT. HALLWAY - NIGHT

She flies down the hall, sobbing - runs faster, but he's gaining on her -

She's almost to the stairs, when--

He reaches out one bloody hand and yanks the sash around her neck -

She falls backward, throws herself at his feet in a clumsy tackle.

He flies forward, over her, down the stairs - CRASH! BOOM! -until he hits bottom - SILENCE.

Trembling, Elizabeth crouches at the top of the stairs and listens ... fearfully creeps down, down, until she can see his body in the darkness -

His badge, glinting in the moonlight, rising, falling steadily.

INT. JAIL - NIGHT

Coulter sleeps in his cell. Micah dips several spoons of brown sugar into his coffee mug. A soft KNOCK comes at the door. He snaps to attention and crosses to the door.

                         MICAH
          Who is it?

                              DORALEE (O.S.)
                    It's me, darlin, Doralee.

He cracks the door open.

The yellow lamplight pours out on Doralee and she smiles,
clutching her shawl around her shoulders.

                              MICAH
                    Sheriff ain't here.

                              DORALEE
                    I ain't lookin' for the sheriff. I'm lookin' for
                    you.

He stares her down. She plunges blithely on.

                              DORALEE
                    I just couldn't sleep, it's so hot tonight. My
                    nightgown is just plain stickin' to me...

She lets her shawl fall open to reveal a thin, clingy nightgown.
After a moment, he steps outside with her, closing the door behind
him.

INT. ELIZABETH'S BEDROOM - NIGHT

Dressed, Elizabeth frantically packs items into her carpetbag -
the photo from her dressing table, a leatherbound book, the parcel
from Jackson's. She sees the cross glinting in the moonlight on
the floor.

She fumbles through a drawer until she finds a ribbon, then ties
the cross around her neck. And is almost out the door when she
remembers -

Grabs the opium and stuffs it into her pocketbook.

EXT. JAIL - NIGHT

Doralee plucks at the low neck of her gown.

                              DORALEE
                    Is Boone Coulter really in there?

                              MICAH
                    What do you want?

                              DORALEE
                    I'm so proud of you, Micah.

She presses up against him and rests her cheek against his chest,

and he's having trouble standing still, not knowing where to put
his hands, or where not to.

> DORALEE
> Is it true, you're gonna get a thousand dollars?

> MICAH
> Two thousand.

Sweet temptation is in his arms and he can hardly breathe.

> DORALEE
> Two thousand dollars! Do you realize what you
> could do, what we could do with two thousand
> dollars?

> MICAH
> (stunned)
> We?

> DORALEE
> I could make you happy, I swear I could. There's
> nuthin for either of us here.

> MICAH
> But - but Doralee -
> (beat)
> You're a whore!

She slugs him - hard.

He grabs his shoulder.

> MICAH
> I - I didn't mean to hurt your feelings.

> DORALEE
> (bitterly)
> How could I ever have expected you to understand?
> You've always had it so easy.

She runs off, crying.

INT. ELIZABETH'S KITCHEN - NIGHT

Elizabeth flings more things into her carpet bag - a loaf of
bread, a few tins of food, a rind of bacon wrapped in cloth.

INT. STAIRCASE - NIGHT

She stands above Dougherty's body. She steels herself and reaches
across him and takes the keys from his belt.

She grabs her cloak from the hall tree and doesn't look back.

EXT. JAIL - NIGHT - A LITTLE LATER

From the shadows between the buildings, Elizabeth steps hesitantly into the street, then rushes to the jail.

Her cloak covers her head, and is fastened securely at her chin, covering her throat.

She edges toward the window and looks in - Micah is sitting at the desk, drinking coffee, studying a piece of paper with his back to her. She clenches her fists in frustration.

INT. JAIL - NIGHT

Micah pulls out a battered old pocket watch and checks the time - 2:00. He stands, stretches, straps on his gun. He shoves his hat on his head and unlocks the door.

He glances back at the cell. Coulter's hat covers his face. Micah exits.

EXT. JAIL - NIGHT

Micah carefully locks the door, tests it, looks in the window - finally hurries down the plank sidewalk to the next building.

From the shadows, Elizabeth watches him test the next door, look around, keep going. When he disappears between buildings, she rushes to the jail door, key in hand, and fumbles with the lock.

INT. DORALEE'S ROOM - NIGHT

Doralee sits alone in her bed, drinking whiskey, staring sadly up at the moon. She picks up the bar of soap and sniffs it longingly.

INT. JAIL - NIGHT

Elizabeth closes the door and falls against it with a trembling sigh -

And sees Coulter stretched out on a pallet in the cell.

Eyes trained on him, she crosses to the desk and tries one of the keys in the desk drawer. It doesn't fit.

She glances up at Coulter; he hasn't moved. She fumbles with more keys until she gets the drawer open.

She reaches inside and pulls out a gun, breaks it open. It's loaded. She slips it into her cloak.

She probes in the drawer again, this time finding the cashbox. She unlocks it, opens it - a few coins.

Desperate, she opens and shuts drawers - and finally covers her face with her hands.

> ELIZABETH
> Oh, Lord, what am I going to do?

Suddenly, she lowers her hands. She slams a drawer. He doesn't move. She looks at the paper on the desk - Coulter's wanted poster. She takes it to the cell.

> ELIZABETH
> Mr. Coulter. I know you're awake.

He pulls the hat away from his face and rises slowly, his eyes clear.

> ELIZABETH
> (checking poster)
> You have killed seven men?

He doesn't speak.

> ELIZABETH
> Two of them lawmen?

Silence.

> ELIZABETH
> And, until today, you were never caught.

She lowers the poster and looks straight into his eyes. He stares back at her.

> ELIZABETH
> I have the key to your cell. I'll release you if
> you agree to my terms.

> COULTER
> What terms?

Swallowing hard, she raises her chin a notch.

> ELIZABETH
> I'm going with you.

He thrusts his hand through the bars.

                    COULTER
        Give me the key.

                    ELIZABETH
        Not yet. The deputy will be back from his rounds
        any time now.

                    COULTER
        I'll take care of the deputy.

                    ELIZABETH
        No! I won't have him hurt. There has to be another
        way.

Coulter clenches his hands on the bars, seething.

                    COULTER
        What the hell other way?

Elizabeth fumbles the bottle of laudanum from her drawstring bag.
She carefully adds drops of laudanum into the cup on the desk.

From the cell, Coulter watches, disbelieving, as Elizabeth stirs
it well.

                    COULTER
        You can't leave me here!

                    ELIZABETH
        I wouldn't dream of it.

She leaves without a backward glance at Coulter. The door CLICKS
locked.

Coulter slams his open palms against the bars.

                    COULTER
        In the name of Jesus!

He paces, boils over - hears a noise outside - Micah enters. He
doesn't notice Coulter. He goes to the window and stares out at
the saloon across the way.

Coulter clears his throat. Micah finally looks at him. Coulter can
hardly force the words out.

                    COULTER
        Can I - can I have a cup of coffee?

EXT. JAIL - NIGHT

Elizabeth eases down the plank walk then presses herself against the wall, peering inside the window.

INT. JAIL - NIGHT

Micah hands Coulter a mug of coffee, careful not to get too close. Coulter doesn't even pretend to drink it. He can only stare at Micah.

Micah sits at the desk and takes one long drag from his own coffee. He dips his finger into the sugar sludge at the bottom and licks it off.

He whistles a bit off key, leans back in his chair, cradles the wanted poster against his chest, slurps some more coffee. Coulter watches in morbid fascination as Micah tries to stand, coughs - then collapses.

INT. DORALEE'S ROOM - NIGHT

Doralee stands in the window looking down on the street. She watches Elizabeth frantically unlock the jail door and rush in.

                    DORALEE
          Holy shit.

She sinks to the floor and props her bottle on the windowsill, still watching.

                    DORALEE
          Wait till the sheriff -

She stops, takes a drink, looks thoughtful.

INT. JAIL - NIGHT

Elizabeth faces Coulter.

                    COULTER
          I think you killed the poor bastard. Hurry up -
          give me the key!

She rushes to Micah's side, peels his eyelid back to check his eyes, nervous, concerned. She adjusts his collar and strokes his cheek.

                    COULTER
          If you don't -

She rises and faces him.

                    ELIZABETH
          You haven't agreed to my terms.

                              COULTER
          You must be in some heap of trouble, lady, and I
          don't think you've got any more time to waste than
          I do. Now just give me the goddamn keys.

Elizabeth tosses him the keys. He reaches through the bars
awkwardly, fumbles, unlocks the padlock, pushes through the
opening -

And meets Elizabeth, training the gun at him.

                             ELIZABETH
          I've just learned something very important about
          you, Mr. Coulter. You don't make promises easily.
          That leads me to believe that when you make them,
          you honor them. That you're a man of your word.
          Now I ask you again, will you take me with you?

He could just about strangle her, probably because she's got him
pegged. Finally, he nods.

                              COULTER
          I'll get you out of town. Now, let's get the hell
          out of here.

                             ELIZABETH
          After you, sir.

                              COULTER
          I told you I'd get you out of town. I work a lot
          better without my own Colt aimed at my vitals.

She lowers the gun.

                             ELIZABETH
          I'm afraid we're going to be together for a little
          longer than you'd like -

                              COULTER
          We already have been.

INT. DORALEE'S ROOM - NIGHT

From the window, she watches Elizabeth lead two horses from the
shadows. Elizabeth and Coulter mount up and take off at a full
gallop.

                             DORALEE
          Well. I'll be damned.

She looks almost awe-struck in admiration.

EXT. DESERT ROAD - NIGHT

The town is a dark silhouette behind them. Coulter cuts off the road and stops. He tosses back his head and lets loose a SHARP WHISTLE.

Nothing responds.

Without a word, he takes off again, this time into the brush. He glances back and sees Elizabeth still following. He looks frustrated and spurs his horse on.

INT. DORALEE'S ROOM - NIGHT

A POUNDING on the door downstairs awakens Doralee from her drunken slumber.

INT. SALOON - NIGHT

She unbars the plank door and opens it to reveal swinging doors on the outside - and nobody there.

EXT. SALOON - NIGHT

Dougherty is slumped against the wall.

                    DORALEE
          Clayton, honey - what - what happened to you?

She pulls him inside the saloon.

INT. SALOON

Doralee shoves a chair under Dougherty as he collapses.

                    DORALEE
          I better get a doctor.

                    DOUGHERTY
          Hell no. No doctor.

                    DORALEE
          Who did this to you?
                    (watches him closely)
          Where's Miz Dougherty?

His expression would curdle milk. She wisely backs down.

                    DORALEE
          Let me put you to bed. In the mornin, you can -

                         DOUGHERTY
          I won't be here in the morning.

But he falls back into the chair and slumps over the table.
Doralee prances nervously at his side.

                         DORALEE
          Clayton, I gotta do somethin. I can't just let you
          ... well, hell!

She whirls out the door.

EXT. JAIL - DAWN

The sky behind her is barely turning pink as Doralee hammers on
the jail door with her fist.

                         DORALEE
          Micah, get your bony ass out here, right now! Wake
          up!

She runs to the window. Inside, Micah is beginning to stir on the
floor. The door to the empty cell is open.

                         DORALEE
                    (mutters)
          I'm gettin' outta this town.

EXT. WILD ROSE CANYON - DAY

Sheer rock walls stretch upward on either side of a dry stream
bed, casting the canyon in shadow as the sun's early rays wash the
opposite wall with fire and gold.

Elizabeth's horse plods steadily along behind Coulter's; she's
doing well to stay mounted. They round a corner in the canyon wall
and the horses splash into a shallow stream.

Coulter dismounts and drops to his knees at the edge, scooping
water into his hands and gulping it down.

Elizabeth grabs the saddle horn with both hands, tries to raise
her leg over and moans.

Coulter turns away from her; his disgust is evident. His sharp
whistle rockets off the canyon walls.

Elizabeth manages to swing down, landing in the water.

She clings to the horse for balance as the water soaks her feet,
her skirt. She collapses to her knees at the edge of the stream
and scoops water desperately into her mouth.

She tugs at the blouse buttoned high on her neck, wincing.

She looks up and catches the outlaw staring at her.

Resentfully, he grabs the saddle horn to mount.

                    ELIZABETH
      Surely we can rest awhile?

His voice is deceptively gentle.

                    COULTER
      You can. Without a horse, and without me.

                    ELIZABETH
      They're - they're probably only now discovering
      we're gone.

Her voice cracks, and she fights to keep the desperation out of
it, but even so, she's pleading.

                    ELIZABETH
      Surely we can spare a few minutes.

                    COULTER
      You're not slowin' me down, you got that? If you
      make it, you make it on your own. I'm not helping
      you.

He swings back onto his horse. Elizabeth drags to her feet.

                    ELIZABETH
      You already have, Mr. Coulter. You saved my life.

Coulter stares at her sullenly, then kicks his horse and rides on,
not waiting to see her haul herself back up on the horse and
follow him.

EXT. A MOUNTAIN SLOPE - DAY

Coulter rides ahead of Elizabeth up the rocky slope.

                    COULTER
      We're about half an hour from that peak. From there
      you can see the town.

                    ELIZABETH
      Where are we going?

                    COULTER
      <u>You're</u> going to Fort Davis.

                              ELIZABETH
          No!

Elizabeth reins the horse into a sharp turn as she tries to change
directions. Coulter grabs its bridle.

                              COULTER
          Just what are you doing?

                              ELIZABETH
          I can't go there!

She grips the reins, tries to break away from him, blinking back
tears, but he won't let go.

                              COULTER
          Lady, you don't have a choice.

                              ELIZABETH
          You don't understand!

                              COULTER
          And I don't want to! You're going to Fort Davis!

                              ELIZABETH
          Nooo!

She thrusts her hand into her saddlebag. But Coulter pulls his
Colt from his holster.

                              COULTER
          Sorry to disappoint you, ma'am, but I relieved you
          of my gun along about sunrise.

He stops short of aiming it at her, but the threat is there.

                              COULTER
          You do what I say, when I say. And I say you're
          going to Fort Davis.

She pulls a pearl-handled derringer from her saddlebag and aims it
straight at his heart.

                              COULTER
          You don't have it in you.

She cocks the pistol.

He stares at her, his expression guarded, not softening. But he
lowers his pistol to his thigh.

                    COULTER
And you sure as hell don't have it in you to go
where I'm going, lady.

                    ELIZABETH
You don't know anything about me.

She clutches the gun in both hands. He shakes his head, disgusted.

                    ELIZABETH
And you don't know anything about ladies.

                    COULTER
I've gotta rest. But come nightfall I'll be rid of
you if I have to leave you tied up on the trail to
El Paso.

                    ELIZABETH
And my husband will kill me.

Coulter laughs, frustrated and incredulous.

                    COULTER
A runaway wife? Well - that figures. What the hell
kind of man is this husband of yours that you're
more afraid of him than of me?!

                    ELIZABETH
He's the kind of man so driven by hatred and
vengeance he'll chase it to the ends of the earth.

                    COULTER
Then lady, this is not your lucky day, because he
sounds a hell of a lot like me.

Elizabeth's gaze never wavers from his as she unties her cloak.

                    ELIZABETH
Maybe so, Mr. Coulter.

She rips open the neck of her blouse. Her throat is purple with
bruises.

                    ELIZABETH
But you never took a vow before God to love me.

His eyes fix on her throat. He remains expressionless.

                    ELIZABETH
Whatever is required of me, Mr. Coulter, I will
endure it. I may be weak, and I may cry too easily,
and I may be too easily swayed by the pretty

                    ELIZABETH (CONT'D)
     praises of men - but I won't ask you to slow down
     again. I won't ask for rest again.
                    (a beat)
     And I won't let you leave me.
                    (buttons her collar)
     Because there are some things I won't endure.

She stares at him, waiting.

                    COULTER
     You just spent more time NOT asking me to slow down
     than when you asked me to slow down. If you're
     going to ride, then just ride.

She almost swoons with relief. He rides off at a swift clip,
leaving her to follow.

EXT. CAMPSITE - NIGHT

A dove COOS and crickets CHIRP. Coulter raises on one elbow. The
horses are ground-staked nearby. Elizabeth sleeps on the ground a
few feet away.

He stares at her, finally kicks his blanket aside and crosses to
the ashes of the fire and fans it...

Then stops, raises his head to listen. Above the night sounds
wafts faint MUSIC, haunting, ghostly, mournful.

He heads cautiously over the mountain top, catching onto mesquites
and junipers to steady himself as he descends the rocky slope on
the other side where he sees...

Scattered camp fires, possibly dozens of them. The night breeze
lifts the MUSIC again, stronger.

The expression on his face is alarmed, yet he creeps closer.

                    UNACCOMPANIED VOICES
     I'm just a poor wayfaring stranger...

Stunned, he misses his footing and skids a little way, freezes,
but nobody calls out or seems to have heard the spray of rocks.

Clinging to a mesquite branch, he stares down at the camp meeting,
his face etched in anguish.

EXT. CAMPSITE - NIGHT

Elizabeth sits nervously at the camp site, shaking drops of
laudanum into water in a tin cup. Rocks CRUNCH and she flings her

head back in time to see Coulter approach. His face is shadowed, gaunt and dark.

                    COULTER
          What are you drinking?

He takes the cup from her hand and sniffs it. He splashes it into the dirt.

                    ELIZABETH
          That was my medicine! I need that!

                    COULTER
          Night riding in the desert is dangerous enough,
          without you riding through it in a daze.

He hands her back her cup. She's rigid with anger.

                    ELIZABETH
          Sometimes the only way to get through life at all
          is in a daze.

He stares at her, incredulous.

                    COULTER
          Is that what you need it for? To numb you?

He laughs bitterly.

                    COULTER
          You should have waited, lady. Life does that to you
          on its own.

He kicks dirt into the small fire, preparing to break camp.

                    COULTER
          We're moving on.

A movement in the shadows. A RUSTLING of brush. He reaches for his gun.

A horse, black as midnight, prances into the campsite. As it spins a wild circle, kicking the air, ugly scars can be seen on its rump.

                    COULTER
          Well. It's about damn time.

EXT. MOUNTAIN TRAIL - NIGHT

Coulter rides Diablo, a task which requires constant gentling of the half-wild horse, constant control.

Elizabeth keeps her distance, but rides doggedly on.

EXT. A MOUNTAIN CREST - DAWN

Elizabeth stands alone on the crest of the mountain. Far below spreads the next stage of their journey: Desert, and on the horizon, more mountains. Her clothes are dirty and wrinkled, her eyes hollow.

Coulter walks up behind her.

> ELIZABETH
> I never knew the world was so vast.

> COULTER
> You carry your own world with you, lady. It's small enough when you've got a hundred rifles aimed at your head.
> (beat)
> I stay high in the mountains when I can, and travel at night and sleep by day. But in this country, there's too much desert. If they catch us, it'll be down there.

> ELIZABETH
> But they won't catch us! They've never caught you before - at least, not until Micah, and that can't count. You were ill.

He stares at her hard.

> COULTER
> And now I've got you.

He picks his way down the slope to the mesquite trees where a tiny campfire burns, leaving Elizabeth to stumble along behind him.

EXT. DAVIS MOUNTAINS CAMPSITE

Elizabeth, alone, digs deep in her carpetbag, pulls out a loaf of stale bread, a tin of tomatoes.

She eases Coulter's leather gloves onto her blistered hands.

She whams one of Coulter's spurs down on the can, and pierces the top again, and again, until she's made a small opening. She inhales, and clutches her stomach in reaction.

She poises to strike again.

From behind her, Coulter grabs the spur. He scowls at a bent point, drops it in the dirt, uses his knife to pry the can open.

She tugs his gloves off, winces, replaces them carefully on his saddlebag. Coulter sees her blisters, but says nothing.

She tears the loaf of bread roughly in half, handing him the larger portion.

Coulter wolfs his down as she nibbles and savors hers.

He pierces a tomato with his knife blade. He eats it, then offers her one on the tip of his knife.

The juice dribbles and squirts as she eats it. He tosses her his grubby bandanna.

She dabs at her chin and neck.

                    COULTER
          Have any sugar for the tomatoes?

                    ELIZABETH
          No, no su-

He's staring at her gaping blouse. She closes it quickly, flushes, manages to stammer -

                    ELIZABETH
          No sugar.

She turns away from him to button her blouse and, embarrassed, realizes he was looking at the cross nestled between her breasts.

Equally embarrassed, he pierces the last small tomato with his knife and holds it out, offering. She shakes her head.

                    COULTER
          My sister had one like it. Your cross.

                    ELIZABETH
          It was a gift from my husband's nephew. It was his
          mother's.

He pops the tomato into his mouth, a trickle of juice running down his neck as he swallows. He starts to wipe his mouth with the back of his hand, but she thrusts the damp bandanna at him.

His hand closes over her wrist and he glares at her, and for a moment neither moves. Then he snatches the bandanna away from her and rubs his mouth dry.

EXT. SAME - DAY

Coulter enters the clearing, leading the horses. Elizabeth sleeps

on a blanket, her cloak covering her.

He drops Diablo's lead and reaches deep into the saddlebag. He pulls out a rectangular bundle bound up in dirty rags, tied with twine.

He sinks to the ground, cradling it in his hands, and rests his forehead against it.

EXT. SITE OF CAMP MEETING, NOW ABANDONED - DAY

Dougherty, Micah and a posse have camped overnight. The posse sits on rocks or squats on their heels near the campfire, drinking coffee uneasily.

Micah sits off to himself, his shoulders slumped in shame. Dougherty stands away from them all, brooding up at the mountains. The wound on his face isn't visible until he turns; then it is brutal.

TWO MEN speak softly to one another, but their voices carry.

                    MAN
          Goddamn Micah - how'd he let Coulter get away? If
          it weren't for him, I'd be home swivvin' my wife.

                    OTHER MAN
          It you don't quit your complainin, I'll swiv ya'
          myself. Nigh on four days now, and ya haven't shut
          up once.

TWO RIDERS approach.

                    FIRST RIDER
          There's been fifty, sixty people through this
          valley in the past week, Sheriff. Reverend Bloys
          held a camp meetin, and they reckon every rancher
          for a hundred miles showed up.

                    DOUGHERTY
          Coulter?

                    FIRST RIDER
          Sorry, sheriff. No sign of anybody resemblin' him
          and Miz Dougherty.

Dougherty turns and stares at the sunwashed slope west of camp.

                    DOUGHERTY
          Reckon you men have come as far as you should have
          to.

The men seem relieved, though cautious not to show it too obviously. But Micah stands.

                    MICAH
        I'm going with you. We'll find him, and get Miz
        Dougherty back.

Dougherty takes the star from his vest and hands it to Micah.

                    DOUGHERTY
        Then you'd better wear this for a while. When I
        find the son-of-a-bitch, I don't want to be a
        lawman.

EXT. DAVIS MOUNTAINS CAMPSITE - DUSK

The sun is dropping low on the horizon. Elizabeth rests her head on her knees, her fists clenched. She raises her face and it's covered with sweat. She stares longingly at her saddlebags.

Slowly, she crawls the few feet to them, and begins searching. She freezes as soft RUSTLINGS come from the underbrush at the edge of the clearing. Coulter breaks out of the brush.

She sits up quickly, nervously watching him.

                    COULTER
        Looking for something?

                    ELIZABETH
        My hairbrush.

She pulls a silverbacked hairbrush out of the saddlebag.

                    COULTER
        Just so it's not your medicine. Once I'm rid of
        you, you can drink the whole damn bottle for all I
        care. But not with me.

                    ELIZABETH
        I was looking for my hairbrush.

He obviously doesn't believe her. He squats to turn a spit with three quail on it. Elizabeth is surprised.

                    ELIZABETH
        I didn't hear gunshots.

                    COULTER
        I snared them.

Agitated, Elizabeth leans her cheek against a tree and stares across the valley.

EXT. THE VALLEY BELOW - DAY

Dougherty is alone, sitting by a small campfire, sharpening his knife. Each stroke is long, loving.

The dry grass near him RUSTLES and he grabs his rifle.

A jackrabbit leaps into the clearing and freezes.

EXT. DAVIS MOUNTAINS CAMPSITE - CONTINUOUS

The distant CRACK echoes faintly. Coulter leaps to his feet and dashes to her side. Elizabeth points at a distant wisp of smoke floating to the sky from the opposite end of the valley.

                         ELIZABETH
          It's just someone hunting for their dinner.

                         COULTER
          How long has that fire been there? Why didn't you
          tell me?

                         ELIZABETH
          I didn't know it mattered.

He closes the distance between them.

                         COULTER
          When you're on the run everything matters!

                         ELIZABETH
          But what about our fire?

                         COULTER
          I built it under a mesquite tree to break up the
          smoke. Now let's get the hell out of here.

He snatches up the quail from the fire.

EXT. CAMPSITE - NIGHT

Micah and Dougherty by a fire. Micah warms his hands. Dougherty drinks from a flask.

                         DOUGHERTY
          Fine Kentucky Bourbon. Try some.

Micah accepts it, takes a swallow, chokes and spews.

                         MICAH
          That's supposed to be good?

Dougherty takes the flask before it spills.

                         DOUGHERTY
          You'll grow into it.

Micah attempts to be casual.

                         MICAH
          What ... what do you know about Doralee?

                         DOUGHERTY
          What's to know about her? She's a whore.

Embarrassed, Micah looks away.

                         MICAH
          Did you ... did you ever tell Doralee about ... me?

                         DOUGHERTY
          Tell her what?

                         MICAH
          About my mother?

                         DOUGHERTY
          Hell, no. What damn business is it of hers?

                         MICAH
                         (sighs)
          Those cuts look like they're festering. Maybe we
          oughta put something on 'em.

                         DOUGHERTY
          Don't worry about 'em.

                         MICAH
          Miz Dougherty'd know what to do.

                         DOUGHERTY
          I said, don't worry about them!

                         MICAH
          I'm sorry. I reckon you're awful worried about her.

Dougherty doesn't say anything, just scowls.

                         MICAH
          What kind of woman turns into a whore? I mean, it
          must be some kind of hurt that would make a woman

do something like that.

                    DOUGHERTY
          Hurt? What the hell are you talking about?

                    MICAH
          I don't know. I'm trying to figure out why women
          do the things they do.

                    DOUGHERTY
          Whores do the things they do because they like
          money and an easy life and they like men.

                    MICAH
          Never seemed that way to me.

Dougherty cuts him a look. But Micah can't drop it.

                    MICAH
          Was that how it was with my mother?

                    DOUGHERTY
          Micah, shut the hell up.

                    MICAH
          Yessir.

EXT. CAMPSITE - DUSK

Coulter is asleep on his bedroll.

                    ELIZABETH (O. S.)
          Don't move.

He opens his eyes and sees her standing a short distance away,
aiming the rifle at him.

He jerks up - A rattlesnake WHIRRRRRS.

He freezes halfway. The rattler snaps into a coil near his head.

He cuts his eyes toward Elizabeth.

The gun is aimed at the snake. He waits.

She tightens her grip, fighting to hold the gun steady.

The snake WHIRRRS.

Without moving a hair - every fiber of him urges her to --

SHOOT!

She doesn't.

He sweats. Swallows.

The snake ... uncoils ... slithers slowly away.

Elizabeth lowers the rifle, trembling.

Coulter springs up and lunges for her -

                    COULTER
          Why didn't you shoot it?

- yanks the rifle away from her, whirls toward where the snake
went - tries to aim - the snake is gone - He spins back to her.

She clenches her trembling hands in front of her. This lady needs
her laudanum - badly.

                    COULTER
          What the hell were you doing?

                    ELIZABETH
          Watching to see what it intended.

He gapes at her, incredulous.

                    COULTER
          Hellfire and damnation - it intended to bite me! I
          said you didn't have it in you to shoot a man, but
          in the name of Jesus, lady you can't even shoot a
          snake?

                    ELIZABETH
          Mr. Coulter - it didn't intend to bite you.

                    COULTER
          How do you claim to know that?

                    ELIZABETH
          I've observed their behavior from my window. I
          enjoy watching the wildlife.

                    COULTER
          From your window.

                    ELIZABETH
          Yes, and if you hadn't moved the snake would never
          have coiled in the first place. I told you not to
          move!

                              COULTER
          Lady, you're not sitting in your big fancy house
          looking out your window - you're living with the
          goddamned snakes, and any goddamn rattler that you
          don't kill is a goddamn rattler that won't give a
          rat's ass about killing you!

Frustrated, she throws her things into her carpetbag.

                              ELIZABETH
          I thought you would be pleased.

If the earth opened up, he couldn't look more astounded.

                              ELIZABETH
          I was trying not to attract attention!

His expression fades a bit.

                              ELIZABETH
          And whether you admit it or not - the snake is
          gone, you didn't get bit, and we haven't fired a
          gun or left a bullet-ridden snake carcass to reveal
          our whereabouts!

He kicks dirt in the fire. Kicks a couple of rocks.

                              COULTER
          Shit.

                              ELIZABETH
          To every thing there is a season, Mr. Coulter. A
          time to kill and a time -

                              COULTER
          Don't quote scripture at me!

He catches himself - calms himself - glares at her.

                              COULTER
          Never quote scripture at a preacher's son.

Now she's astounded.

                              COULTER
          It'll backfire on you, every time. Especially when
          it comes to women and snakes.

EXT. DESERT - NIGHT

Coulter and Elizabeth ride through a sea of eerie gray creosote
bushes that seem to stretch forever.

He rides relentlessly ahead, but Elizabeth is barely staying astride her horse, hunched over in agony.

She slumps forward and the mare stutter-steps.

Coulter glances back, sees her sliding sideways-

                         COULTER
        Damn it!

He leaps from his saddle and catches her as she falls.

He holds her, stunned, her cloak billowing around them both, her head hanging limply. Chills wrack her body.

                         COULTER
        Mercy, lady. How much of that juice had you been
        taking?

He grabs a canteen and eases her to the ground. He lifts her head into his lap to drink, but the water dribbles down her chin. He nudges her lips apart with a finger and dribbles water into her mouth.

At first nothing - then she swallows a bit. A little more, a little more, his fingers damp with moisture as he keeps easing water into her mouth.

She moans softly, stirs, coughs.

She turns her face into his belly. His hand cradles the back of her head, even as he strains his body away from her. He dribbles more water in her mouth.

Her eyes open. She clutches at him but he pulls completely away, letting her ease onto the dirt. Her eyes close again. He looks off to the east at the faint pink glow of dawn.

After a moment, he scoops her into his arms and crosses to Diablo. He mounts, and mouth set in a rigid line, he holds her against him as he moves on.

INT. REDEMPTION SALOON - NIGHT

Doralee sits forlornly alone - but clean. She dips her finger into a glass of whiskey and sucks it off.

From the bar, OLIVER P. WINSTON watches her. He's a Yankee dandy who has made no effort to fit in the West.

Winston pulls up a chair, startling her. He pours a splash of her
whiskey into his glass, and nods, amused.

                    WINSTON
          Just as I thought. The rotgut they sold me wasn't
          their best. I'm Oliver P. Winston. I write for
          Harper's Weekly.

                    DORALEE
          There ain't nothing around Redemption worth writin'
          about.

She flicks a finger at the bartender, who brings another glass as
they continue talking, Doralee melting with suggestive charm,
scratching deep in her bodice, lowering her neckline in the
process.

                    WINSTON
          Maybe not any more, miss, but-

                    DORALEE
          Doralee. You can call me Doralee.

                    WINSTON
          Doralee...

His lips seem to enjoy tasting the name as much as his eyes enjoy
the view down her cleavage.

                    WINSTON
          Doralee ... it seems that quite a tale is brewing
          here. One of the most violent, murdering outlaws
          known kidnaps the very proper sheriff's wife - yes,
          I can see the story selling newspapers from San
          Francisco to Baltimore.

                    DORALEE
          Boone Coulter, Boone Coulter! All a body ever hears
          about these days is that no good louse Boone
          Coulter.

                    WINSTON
          You know him?

                    DORALEE
          No, and I don't want to. The only way I was
          interested in that gentleman was to see him
          twitchin' at the end of a noose.

                    WINSTON
          Strong opinion for someone who doesn't even know
          the man.

                         DORALEE
     He was gonna provide me with a new life, that's
     all.

                         WINSTON
     By hanging?

                         DORALEE
     Given a little more time, I would've had a piece of
     his reward money.

                         WINSTON
     Now just exactly how ...?

                         DORALEE
     Let's just say I'm personally acquainted with the
     man who did the capturin'.

                         WINSTON
     Lucky man.

She stands up, giving him a clear view down her bosom as she leans
over him and pulls him to his feet.

                         DORALEE
     If it's information you're after, you've come to
     the right place.

                         WINSTON
     And what would you expect in return for this
     information?

                         DORALEE
     Passage on the first stage out of this shit hole.

                         WINSTON
     Miss Doralee, I do believe we could work out an
     arrangement.

                         DORALEE
     And money to spare.

                         WINSTON
     That can be arranged.

Her smile is beatific. His is appreciative.

EXT. DESERT SALT FLAT - DAY

Coulter rides around the edge of the salt flats beneath the grim
Sierra Diablos, a wall of cliffs a thousand feet high. He holds
Elizabeth's sweat-soaked body in his arms.

His lips are parched, but he dribbles the last of the water into her mouth. He urges the horse on.

INT. COULTER'S CABIN - NIGHT

Elizabeth rolls her head to the side. A mug is near her face. She reaches for it, falls back in pain.

On the other side of the cabin, Coulter stokes the fire. He drops his stick and rises to go to her.

Not seeing him, she drinks from the mug, spilling most of it. She falls back and closes her eyes.

Coulter sinks back to his haunches, his back to the fire, maintaining his weary vigil.

                                              DISSOLVE TO:

INT. COULTER'S CABIN - NIGHT

Elizabeth jerks upright, clutching the imaginary sash at her throat, ripping at the neck of her blouse.

                         ELIZABETH
          No ... no ... please!

Coulter springs to her side. She claws him, fights for her life. He catches her arms at her sides, wraps his around her, holds her until her until it passes.

She falls limp, lost in her nightmare, unaware of him. The cross at her neck glints in the moonlight.

                                              DISSOLVE TO:

INT. COULTER'S CABIN - DAY

In the gray dawn Elizabeth sleeps, her arm hanging off the bed and her hand resting softly against -

Coulter, stretched out an the dirt floor beside her.

Thunder RUMBLES in the distance.

INT. COULTER'S CABIN - DAY

Wind whips the shuttered windows behind Elizabeth's head. Rain LASHES the roof in sheets.

She awakens slowly, touches her throat, winces. She seems to focus slowly, registers confusion and panic, looks around the one-room

cabin to find - Coulter standing in the doorway, watching the
rain.

                    ELIZABETH
          Thank God.

Coulter whips around to face her, his expression guarded. He's
exhausted.

                    ELIZABETH
          I thought you were - I thought I was alone.

She struggles to her feet, but loses her balance.

                    COULTER
          Sit down before you keel over again.

She sits. He brings her coffee, avoiding her eyes.

                    ELIZABETH
          Where are we?

                    COULTER
          A place I stay sometimes.

                    ELIZABETH
          Where is that?

                    COULTER
          The less you know, the better I like it.

She lowers the coffee to her lap.

                    ELIZABETH
          You think I'd betray you?

                    COULTER
          You said it. If you needed to.

                    ELIZABETH
          We've got that in common, I suppose.

                    COULTER
          No. We don't.

                    ELIZABETH
          But the men you've killed.

                    COULTER
          That had nothing to do with living.

Thunder CRASHES overhead. Elizabeth jumps, a flash of her night terror crossing her face.

Coulter turns to the fire, his back to her.

> COULTER
> The bacon's cooked, and a rabbit stewed. I've got
> to get some sleep.

Elizabeth sinks back on the bed, staring in confusion as he grabs
a blanket and goes outside.

INT. CABIN - NIGHT

The rain has stopped. Elizabeth watches through the window as
Coulter sleeps huddled under a tree.

INT. CABIN - DAY

Dirty, disheveled, Elizabeth digs through her carpetbag until she
finds the brown package from Jackson's store. She tears it open
to find -

A tin of Egyptian henna. Dismayed, she rolls it back into the
paper and shoves it deep into the bag.

She takes the lye soap from the hearth.

EXT. PATH FROM STREAM - DAY

Elizabeth walks up the path, her damp hair loose, reading a small
book. Coulter emerges from the bushes - they collide, the book
hits the dirt.   She lunges for it, but he's faster than she is.
Embarrassed, she holds out her hand. He reads the page, frowns.

> ELIZABETH
> Have you ever read Keats? Ode to a Grecian Urn?

> COULTER
> A jar? Hell of a thing to write a poem about.

He returns the book and starts to push past her.

> ELIZABETH
> No - not about the jar. About the people trapped
> in it, circling it, chasing each other forever. I
> would think you'd know how that felt, being
> trapped. Frozen.

He just shakes his head and edges past her. Finally she walks on,
slowly.

EXT. STREAM - DAY

Coulter watches her walk up the path, her hair catching sunlight. He slumps against the maple tree, his eyes squeezed shut.

INT. COULTER'S CABIN - NIGHT

Combing her hair she stops in midstroke, spying something across the room. She glances at the cabin door.

She crosses the room and takes Coulter's cloth-wrapped bundle from the shelf above the fireplace. She opens it.

It's a Bible. She checks the door again, then turns pages until she finds the family registry in the middle.

She runs her finger down the list of names, births, deaths ... and closes it, frowning. She hears something - hurriedly puts it back.

INT. COULTER'S CABIN - DUSK

Coulter appears in the doorway. It is almost dark behind him. Elizabeth is seated on the bed.

                    COULTER
          I'm leaving in the morning.

                    ELIZABETH
          What?

                    COULTER
          I have unfinished business.

                    ELIZABETH
          I'll go with you.

She struggles to her feet, her hands outstretched in entreaty.

                    COULTER
          Look at your palms. You've gone as far as you can.

Elizabeth begins laughing hysterically.

                    ELIZABETH
          You've brought me into the middle of godforsaken
          nowhere and you're going to abandon me?

                    COULTER
          This time of year folks pass through every few
          weeks, or so. I'm sure you'll have no difficulty
          convincing someone else to help you.
                    (pointedly)
          I'll leave you your gun.

                    ELIZABETH
Other people know where you live? And you trust
them not to betray you?

                    COULTER
I don't trust anybody. There are a handful of
people on this earth who know where I live, and
fewer still know who I am. Nobody knows both.

                    ELIZABETH
But I know. Who you are, and where you hide.

                    COULTER
Shit.

                    ELIZABETH
Like it or not, you have to trust me, don't you?

                    COULTER
I leave at dawn, and you're staying. I don't
intend to be looking over my shoulder for your
husband every step of the way.

She sinks to the bed and looks away from him. Suddenly suspicious,
he studies her.

                    COULTER
Or is that what you wanted all along? An easy way
to get rid of that wedding band.

Startled, she slips her ring off her finger, then slowly slides it
back on, then off, then back on, as if hypnotized by the movement,
or by the thought.

                    COULTER
You want him to come after me, or me to go after
him. You want me to kill your husband.

                    ELIZABETH
How could you say - of course not!

She stares up at him, afraid.

                    ELIZABETH
Is that what I want? Dear God in heaven, is that
what this is all about?

                    COULTER
I think you just answered your own question, lady.
You thought I was gonna bust that jar.

INT. CABIN - NIGHT

Elizabeth stares into the blackness, weeping silently. The wind rattles the boarded window behind her head.

EXT. CABIN - NIGHT

Coulter stands alone at the edge of the clearing, facing into the HOWLING wind. A muffled CRASH comes from the cabin.

He sprints for the open door.

INT. CABIN - CONTINUOUS

On the bed, Elizabeth fights to close the shutter. Coulter pushes her aside and slams it shut. He shoves a wooden slat in place.

Elizabeth scoots to the end of the bed, tugging her camisole strap to cover herself.

                    COULTER
      Are you hurt?

Her back is to him, her fist at her mouth.

                    COULTER
      Let me see.

His hand closes over her bare shoulder.

They both freeze.

He tries to pull his hand away, but she catches it, holds it against her. His eyes lock with hers in tense silence. Slowly, he begins stroking his thumb across her collarbone.

Until she can't restrain the impulse to turn her head and press her lips against the back of his hand.

He jerks away, his voice tight, strangled.

                    COULTER
      You don't know what you're doing.

She faces him, then, slowly raises on her knees.

                    ELIZABETH
      But I do.

She takes his hand and kisses his palm. He flinches. She places his hand over her heart.

He slides it to her breast, his body rigid.

She unbuttons her camisole, her eyes never leaving his. She raises her chin in challenge, leaving the fabric hanging loosely, only a whisper of skin showing... and she waits.

When he finally moves, he doesn't part her blouse. He brushes her hair away and gazes at her throat and his eyes flinch with pain. And when he bends closer, it isn't her lips he seeks, but the dark bruises on her neck that he kisses so gently.

She flings her head back, leans into him. Their bodies melt together. His hands burrow under her camisole.

His mouth finds hers, fusing, tasting, exploring - until she gasps and pulls back and meets his startled, hungry expression.

                    COULTER
          I hurt you.

                    ELIZABETH
          Mr. Coulter - leave me now, and I swear I will die.

He bends closer, his lips brushing hers.

                    COULTER
          I should. I should stop. I should leave tonight -

She silences him with a hard kiss. She tunnels her fingers into his hair and pulls him down on her.

                                        DISSOLVE TO:

INT. CABIN - NIGHT

Coulter's head is on her shoulder, his eyes closed, as he sleeps. Elizabeth stares into the dark; a tear rolls down her cheek.

INT. CABIN - DAWN

Coulter is startled to awaken beside her. Hesitantly, he leans closer, inhales deeply of her hair.

He draws a shuddering breath, rolls away from her, and pulls on his trousers.

                    ELIZABETH
          Mr. Coulter.

She watches him from the bed.

                    ELIZABETH
          I want you to know, about last night - I'm not
          sorry.

                    COULTER
     I am.

He yanks his boots on, snatches up his shirt and spins toward the
door, but stops.

                    COULTER
     I don't steal. That goes for other men's wives,
     too.

                    ELIZABETH
     I'm not a piece of goods! I don't belong to any
     man and certainly not to Clayton Dougherty!

Coulter stares at her.

                    COULTER
     Clayton Dougherty? Is your husband?

She rises, clutching the blanket across her breasts.

                    ELIZABETH
     How dare you look so long-suffering, so guilt-
     ridden! You didn't steal anything and - and I
     didn't offer myself to you as payment - I took
     comfort from you, and, and tenderness, because I
     needed it.

                    COULTER
     And if I had needed it? If I were the one doing the
     taking, you'd sing a different song.

He storms out the door.

EXT. CABIN - DAY

Coulter throws his head back, gives a sharp WHISTLE, and heaves
his saddle to his shoulder. Diablo WHINNIES in the distance.

Elizabeth appears in the cabin doorway clutching his shirt closed
over her own white lawn drawers.

                    ELIZABETH
     Just in case you've forgotten, If it weren't for
     me, you'd be swinging from a rope!

                    COULTER
     God!

He slings the saddle to the ground.

                    COULTER
What do you want from me?!

                    ELIZABETH
Not a thing.

She turns to go back inside, but he grabs her arm and pulls her
back.

                    COULTER
The hell you say!

                    ELIZABETH
You've already lost two hours of daylight. I'll not
have you blaming me for that, too. Just go!

She tries to pull away but he won't let her. The hand that
slithers into her hair and jerks her to him is not gentle. His
eyes are cold, lethal. His kiss is crushing, devouring. She
fights him.

                    COULTER
Isn't this what you wanted, Lady Elizabeth? Isn't
this what you need to survive?

                    ELIZABETH
No!

He kisses her again, his hands roaming her back, pulling her to
him. She isn't fighting any more.

                    COULTER
You've broken all the rules that kept me away from
you. You broke them, Mrs. Dougherty. Tell me to
stop. Tell me this isn't what you want.

                    ELIZABETH
Why are you doing this?

                    COULTER
Because this is what you did to me.

                    ELIZABETH
That's a lie! I offered you as much as I took. I
didn't take without caring!

He clutches her shoulders, glares down at her.

                    COULTER
What the hell made you think I didn't care?

He shoves her away as Diablo trots into the clearing.

Stunned, Elizabeth watches him heave his saddle to his shoulder and stalk toward the horse.

He stops, tension radiating from him like heat from the desert.

He flings his saddle to the ground, slaps Diablo on the rump. His fists clenched, he turns, sees her in the doorway as the horse gallops away.

                    COULTER
          If you knew what Clayton Dougherty did to me - if
          you knew what a taste I have for vengeance - you're
          a fool if you give me a chance to take an eye for
          an eye.

He closes the distance between them, takes her in his arms, kisses her with a deepfelt hunger.

EXT. BRUSH - DAY

Elizabeth carefully picks her way into the brush and trees. She watches every step, uses a stick to thwack the bushes. She finds a clear place and ...

Lifts her skirts and squats.

A rattlesnake's WHIRRRRRR....

She freezes.

Silence.

Terrified, she moves only her eyes, checks around her - nothing.

She can't move. Can't breathe. Just squats.

EXT. CABIN - DAY

Coulter peers back into the brush. Tends the fire. Looks up at the sky. Looks back into the brush.

Finally, Elizabeth emerges from the brush, shaking, hyperventilating.

                    COULTER
          You okay?

She nods briskly. Barely manages to walk - not run -to the cabin.

As she reaches the door, Coulter says ...

                              COULTER
          M'lady.

She spins to face him. He leans against a boulder nonchalantly,
and with his mouth ....

WHIRRRRRRRRRSSSS.

She huffs into the cabin and slams the door.

He catches himself grinning - and stiffens.

INT. CABIN - CONTINUOUS

Heaving for breath - she silently rages - then covers her mouth
when she starts to laugh.

A quick look at the door - she digs deep into her carpet bag and
brings out the tiny vial of perfume. Touches one single drop to
the pulse of her throat, then embarrassed, shoves it back deep
into the bag, and watches the door -

Coulter enters. Doesn't look at her. Braces his hands against
the mantle, on either side of the bundle-wrapped Bible.

Her expectancy fades into confusion.

                              COULTER
          I'm taking you to Seven Rivers in the morning.

And shock. And anger.

                              ELIZABETH
          I refuse. Not if it will put you in greater
          danger, and it will.

                              COULTER
          Greater danger? As if you haven't done that
          already?

She draws back. Simmers. Points at the Bible on the mantle.

                              ELIZABETH
          Tell me. Where did you get that Bible?

He snaps a look from the Bible to her, and his eyes narrow.

                              COULTER
          You've been going through my things? You have no
          right!

                    ELIZABETH
          It's not yours. How did you get it?

                    COULTER
          What the hell are you talking about?

                    ELIZABETH
          That's Micah's family Bible!

                    COULTER
          Micah?

                    ELIZABETH
          Micah Bridges.

He stares at her, not breathing.

                    ELIZABETH
          Clayton's deputy. His nephew.

He sinks onto the bed, the Bible in his hands, his face turned to
stone.

                    ELIZABETH
          What is it? What is going on?

He glares at her.

                    COULTER
          When you broke me out of jail, you took your
          chances. You probably got more than you bargained
          for, but no more than you deserved. And you don't
          deserve any answers.

                    ELIZABETH
          I deserve to know what connects you to Micah - and
          to my husband!

Coulter steps toward her, his voice suddenly smooth, measured,
chilling.

                    COULTER
          It's really very simple. A long time ago my sister
          fell in love with a young buck who had money. Joel
          Dougherty.

Elizabeth recoils.

                    ELIZABETH
          Joel?

Coulter gives her a hard look. His laughter is bitter.

                         COULTER
    Why aren't I surprised? Joel would've been more
    your type. So maybe you owe me a story, too?

She rises, paces to the window.

                         ELIZABETH
    Please ...

                         COULTER
    Turnabout's fair play.

Unwavering, Coulter settles back to listen.

                         ELIZABETH
    I knew Joel. Well. Too well.
                    (a beat)
    When I came to Texas, he wasn't waiting for me,
    despite his sweet seductions. I can't blame him.
    It's one thing to seduce a lonely woman. Quite
    another to marry one.

Coulter frowns, taken aback.

                         ELIZABETH
    That's why Clayton could never forgive me for not
    being what he thought I was when he married me.

                         COULTER
    Then why the hell--

                      __ ELIZABETH
    Because he offered, Mr. Coulter. Because he
    offered.

She dares him to judge her.

                         ELIZABETH
    I believe it's your turn.

He meets her gaze, fire with fire.

                         COULTER
    My parents and my baby brother were burned alive in
    our cabin when my pa started to preach abolition
    and folks didn't want to hear it. Clayton Dougherty
    threw the first torch.

That takes the starch out of her.

                         ELIZABETH
    No. My God, no.

                         COULTER
They weren't supposed to be there. It was a night
when my pa was preaching, and the cabin would have
been empty. But my brother was sick, and my mother
and Susannah stayed home with him.

Elizabeth gasps. He just looks at her.

                         COULTER
Yes, Susannah. My sister.

                        ELIZABETH
Micah's mother.

                         COULTER
My father and I got home in time to find the cabin
in flames. I got Susannah out - barely. My father
went after the others and got trapped and -

He gathers himself.

                         COULTER
Joel wouldn't marry her - couldn't bear looking at
her face. At the scars his brother gave her.

He steps even closer, his face like stone but his eyes burning
with anger.

                         COULTER
And just in case you decide there's anything else
you deserve to know, John Wesley Bridges died with
them that day, so do us both a favor and don't go
trying to find him.

Elizabeth walks to the door, and their backs are to each other.

                        ELIZABETH
And Susannah?

                         COULTER
Became a whore. Lived in a haze of opium for
years, hiding from the world, especially from me.
                    (beat)
After she died, I found out she'd had a baby. Joel
Dougherty's son.

Stricken, Elizabeth clutches the cross at her neck.

                         COULTER
I never saw him, never knew anything except that
she found a home for him. But I never dreamed - in
my worst nightmares - she'd hand him over to

Clayton Dougherty.

                    ELIZABETH
She kept him with her as long as she could, long
enough that Micah remembers, and suffers for it.
She wrote and begged Joel to come get him and give
him a decent life...Joel did not go.

She stares sadly into the distance, into the past.

                    ELIZABETH
But Clayton went. He rescued the boy. He said
Micah was his blood, his responsibility. I like to
think I wouldn't have married him, had I not
thought he had a sense of honor.

                    COULTER
Lady, has it ever occurred to you that you have a
weakness for men with guilty consciences?

                    ELIZABETH
If that were truly so, I'd be madly in love with my
husband.

                    COULTER
I'm taking you to Seven Rivers. Then I'll finish
what I should have done years ago.

INT. EL PASO NEWSPAPER OFFICE - DAY

Micah and Dougherty enter. Dougherty goes to the counter.

A CLERK rushes up with a bundle of handbills.

                    CLERK
Hot off the presses, Mr. Dougherty.

The clerk opens the package and proudly presents a page.
Dougherty's scowl fades.

                    CLERK
I never seed such a good likeness.

Dougherty folds it carefully and places it in his jacket.

                    CLERK
Boss said tell ya it was a pleasure, and we hope
you find yer wife.

EXT. CARLSBAD, NEW MEXICO JAIL - DAY

We see the back of a man's shoulder: LUCIUS MERRIWEATHER, a black mountain man. Beyond him on the wall is a tattered assortment of wanted posters. A new one stands out, our view of it partially blocked by Lucius's shoulder. Only visible is the bold word across the top: "KIDNAPPED."

He rips the poster from the wall.

INT. COULTER'S CABIN - NIGHT

From high above we look down on Coulter and Elizabeth on the rope bed, back to back, perfectly and quietly still as if sleeping. But slowly, Elizabeth rolls over and eases her hand across Coulter's waist. We move closer, and see the apprehension on her face, until she knows he's asleep and she relaxes against his back and closes her eyes.

We follow her arm, draped across his middle, to her hand, cupped against his stomach, and slowly, slowly, up his body until we see his eyes, awake, staring at her hand. He closes them, grimaces and swallows hard, opens them, and stares into the night.

A bird call TRILLS outside. Coulter stares more intently. After a few moments, it TRILLS again. Coulter eases himself away from Elizabeth and, grabbing his gunbelt, moves silently toward the door. He presses himself flat against the wall and peers out, his gun raised.

Through the door we see a hulking silhouette at the edge of the clearing.

EXT. CABIN - NIGHT

The bird call TRILLS again, and before it finishes, Coulter is out the door, whispering.

                    COULTER
     Lucius?

                    LUCIUS
     Johnny!

Lucius Merriweather closes the distance between them and wraps Coulter in a crushing bear hug, despite the pistol now wavering dangerously near his head.

                    LUCIUS
          Put that firearm down, friend!

Lucius barrels toward the cabin but stops at the door, seeing Elizabeth sleeping.

                         LUCIUS
          Lordy, lordy ...

Coulter pulls him away from the door.

                         COULTER
          We can talk out here.

Coulter drops to his heels and leans against the cabin.

Lucius hunkers down with him. He reaches in his shirt pocket and
pulls out a pouch and rolls a cigarette.

                         COULTER
          How'd you know I was here?

                         LUCIUS
          Jest had a feelin', that's all.

He lights the cigarette and gives Coulter a sidelong glance in the
flare of the match.

                         LUCIUS
          Didn't know you had company.

Coulter doesn't respond, and Lucius shakes the match out and
tosses it aside. Finally asks pointblank.

                         LUCIUS
          Who is she?

                         COULTER
          Somebody in trouble.

Lucius grunts and smokes in silence, flicks the ash off the end of
his cigarette.

                         LUCIUS
          Some strange goings on down southwest of here.

He pulls a folded, dirty paper from inside his shirt. He tosses it
to Coulter, watching him closely.

Coulter stares at the open paper in his hand.

                         LUCIUS
          These things are all over. I've seed 'em in every
          town I've passed through fer the past week, I
          reckon.

Coulter folds the poster, offers it back to Lucius. Lucius refuses
it with a wave of his cigarette.

LUCIUS
Most people tend to leave killers alone, especially
when they think the killin's over some kind of
private business between two fellers who likely as
not deserve what they're gettin. But kidnap an
innocent woman and folks get stirred up. Take a
pretty damn fool kind of idiot to do a thing like
that, wouldn't you reckon?

COULTER
If that's what he did.

LUCIUS
Ya don't have any reason to doubt it, do ya,
Johnny?

COULTER
I'm beginning to think I could believe about
anything.

LUCIUS
Think I'll sleep down by the stream. I always did
like the sound of water. Ain't enough of it around
here for nothin, might as well enjoy it while I
can.

Coulter stands, and Lucius lumbers to his feet and tosses the
cigarette butt to the ground, grinds it out with his boot.

LUCIUS
Fact is, there ain't much reason to hang 'round
these parts much longer. I just thought I'd let ya
know bout them posters.

Coulter waits for him to leave the clearing before turning to
enter the cabin.

INT. CABIN - NIGHT

Elizabeth is standing by the fire, waiting for him when he enters.
Her voice trembles.

ELIZABETH
Who is that man?

COULTER
Lucius Merriweather. He's a mountain man. Wanders
through here once or twice a year.

Agitated, she moves about the cabin, not meeting his eyes as he stokes the fire, lifts the coffee pot and moves it closer to heat.

                    ELIZABETH
          So they're saying you kidnapped me.

                    COULTER
          Go back to sleep. There's nothing to be done about
          it now.

She pulls her hairbrush from her saddlebag, glances over her
shoulder to see if he's watching as she reaches deeper into the
bag. He tests the coffee with his finger, finds it not hot enough
and puts it back.

She stares at him through haunted eyes.

                    ELIZABETH
          There's enough coffee for all of us. You should
          take some to your friend.

Coulter looks a little exasperated, but nods, filling a tin mug.

Elizabeth waits till he's outside then pulls the bottle of
laudanum from the folds of her skirt. She doses his mug and rushes
to put the vial back in her bag. She stirs coffee into the mug.

                    ELIZABETH
          Please forgive me.

She looks up to find him standing in the doorway, his expression
soft, worried.

He crosses the room to her. For the first time we see a gesture of
uninhibited tenderness as he caresses her shoulder and sweeps a
strand of hair away from her face, which is almost her undoing.
Her hand trembles so violently she almost drops the cup. He takes
the cup out of her hand and places it on the table.

                    ELIZABETH
          I can't - bear the thought that you'll be hurt, and
          it'll be my fault.

He kisses her, full and warm and tender, and she melts against
him, and if ever we were to believe that everything could be all
right, this is the time.

But when she turns her face toward us her eyes are wide open and
haunted. And when she speaks, her voice is barely audible.

                    ELIZABETH
          Your coffee is getting cold, Mr. Coulter.

INT. CABIN - NIGHT

She stands at the mantel and places Joel's photograph beside the Bible. She takes the cross from her neck and loops it over the photo and Bible, not bothering to wipe her tears.

INT. CABIN - DAWN

Coulter awakens, squinting, holding his head in pain, raises up to see that he's alone in the bed.

He tries to stand, and falls forward, catches himself on the table, sees the mug overturned on the floor.

He drops to his knees and snatches the mug up, sniffs it, and his face contorts in rage.

EXT. MOUNTAIN TRAIL - DAY

Gray dawn, steady rain pelting Elizabeth's face as she rides beside Lucius across the desert plain. The mountains loom dark behind them.

                    LUCIUS
          We've been in New Mexico Territory for an hour or
          so.

Huddled in her sodden cloak, Elizabeth manages a nod.

                    LUCIUS
          Wetter year than we've had in recent memory. Never
          complain about rain, though, less'n it sweeps away
          yer missus and kids. Then maybe you've got
          something to complain about. Maybe.

Elizabeth looks back over her shoulder.

                    ELIZABETH
          How long will it take us to get to Seven Rivers?

                    LUCIUS
          A day and a half, maybe longer.

He angles his head up at the sky, not minding the rain.

                    LUCIUS
          Then again, maybe not.

                    ELIZABETH
          Do you ever give a straight answer?

                    LUCIUS
        All my answers are straight. It's my mind that
        wanders here and yon. No sooner do I reckon one
        thing than another comes along to distract me.

He reaches into his saddlebag, digs around.

                    LUCIUS
        Jest like last night. When you asked me to help you
        get to Seven Rivers, I figured it was a good thing.
        Johnny's done been through too much to risk it all
        for something I could do just as well. He's a good
        boy, Johnny is, no matter what he done.

Elizabeth shoots a startled glance at him. He's eyeing her as
well. He hands her a Mexican poncho. She accepts it dubiously and
slips it over her head.

                    LUCIUS
        Now that I've done got in the middle of it, I
        wonder if I made a mistake. Always suspected
        Johnny was the kind of man I wouldn't want to be on
        the wrong side of.

                    ELIZABETH
        It had to be done.

                    LUCIUS
        I just don't want to be the one to explain why,
        that's for sure.

                    ELIZABETH
        No one will have to explain anything, Mr.
        Merriweather. He'll understand.

                    LUCIUS
        If that don't beat all. Every time you call me
        that, I feel like lookin over my shoulder to see
        who the fine gentleman is.

He laughs, and she smiles back.

                    LUCIUS
        You've a mighty fine seat on a horse, fer all that
        you're a lady and all.

Again she shoots him a startled look, but he only kicks up his
horse's speed, leaving her to follow.

EXT. CABIN - DAY

Coulter stumbles out into the clearing, his eyes wild.

                          COULTER
        Lady!

He staggers to the place where the mare was tethered and finds the
rope on the ground, follows the tracks down toward the stream,
where another set joins them.

                          COULTER
        Lucius?

He whirls and shouts, his voice rocketing off the canyon walls

                          COULTER
        NO!

He begins running back toward the cabin and whistles sharply,
waits, whistles again, hears a distant NEIGH.

EXT. OUTSIDE OF SEVEN RIVERS - NIGHT

The sky is filled with stars and Lucius and Elizabeth stand by
their horses.

                          LUCIUS
        I know you need a good bed tonight, but we've gotta
        do this careful.

                          ELIZABETH
        Tonight I'll find a blanket and the hard ground a
        blessing, if I don't have to share it with a
        rattler or a prickly pear.

                          LUCIUS
        When we ride into town in the morning, we're gonna
        tie your head in a scarf and wrap that robe around
        your shoulders just so.

                          ELIZABETH
        Surely you don't think they'll believe I'm an
        Indian.

                          LUCIUS
        Nope. Just a rancher's wife, down on her luck.
        That means that fine wool cloak'll be folded in
        your bag. And your way of speaking. Can't dirty
        that up or cover it up, so's I guess the safest
        thing is for you to keep your mouth shut.

A star streaks across the sky.

                          LUCIUS
        Looky there! A shooting star. Reckon that means

luck. Less'n it don't signify on account of the
Tears of Saint Lawrence 'n all.

She raises her head, but she's too late to see it.

> LUCIUS
> Every year this time, the sky's full of 'em. A
> little early, though.
> So maybe that one does count for luck.

He spits at the ground.

> LUCIUS
> Then again, maybe not.

INT. SEVEN RIVERS MERCANTILE - DAY

Elizabeth stands at a counter beside Lucius Merriweather.

Her dirty clothes, the Indian blanket poncho, make her look
disreputable. The STOREKEEPER eyes them warily.

> STOREKEEPER
> What kind of jewelry would the madam care to
> dispose of?

His expression changes to pity when she slips her wedding band
from her finger.

> STOREKEEPER
> Good gold, but not worth an awful lot.

> LUCIUS
> I heard you was honest, or I wouldn't have brung
> her here. Don't make me a liar.

> STOREKEEPER
> I'd no sooner take advantage of this poor widow
> woman than - I'm sorry, I can't offer much.

> LUCIUS
> Enough for a ticket on the Albuquerque stage?

Elizabeth can't stand there any longer and leaves them to haggle.

> STOREKEEPER
> I think I can manage that.

> LUCIUS
> We're much obliged.

                    STOREKEEPER
          I'm sorry about her husband.

EXT. MERCANTILE - DAY

She takes a seat at the edge of the bench. Lucius joins her.

                      LUCIUS
          I wish I could have gotten you a little extra.

                    ELIZABETH
          You've been a true friend.

                      LUCIUS
          Stage is due about noon. Maybe you won't have to
          wait too long. Then again--

                    ELIZABETH
          Maybe I will.

He grins down at her. But she's looking south down the main
street, watching nervously.

                      LUCIUS
          Stage'll be coming from the other direction.

                    ELIZABETH
          I'm not looking for the stage.

EXT. SEVEN RIVERS - DAY

Riding into town, Coulter and his mount are a worn, bedraggled
pair, the horse lathered, Coulter, dirty, unshaven, narrow-eyed
and sullen.

A woman in a dark cloak stands in front of the Mercantile, her
hand shielding her eyes from the sun.

Coulter digs his heels into his horse, gallops the last way and is
off the horse even before it completely stops. But the woman
turns to face him - a stranger. She beckons to a man with a wagon.

Coulter stares blindly after her, then enters the store.

INT. MERCANTILE

Coulter pushes past a customer.

                     COULTER
          The stage ... when's it due?

The storekeeper continues measuring out a length of calico, an arm's length from his nose.

> STOREKEEPER
> Won't be another one until next Thursday. You
> missed it by a day.

> COULTER
> Missed it? Did a woman get on? A woman alone?

The storekeeper rips the fabric off.

> STOREKEEPER
> A widow from a ranch out east of here. One of her
> husband's men saw her off.

Coulter drags his fingers through his hair, then suddenly raises
his head.

> COULTER
> What did the man look like?

> STOREKEEPER
> Colored man. Big fellow.

> COULTER
> Where is that stage headed?

> STOREKEEPER
> Albuquerque, Santa Fe, Cimarron.

Coulter is already headed out the door.

EXT. MERCANTILE - DAY

He ducks his head in the horse trough to clear it, and mounts his
horse and pushes on.

EXT. STAGE COACH - DAY

The stage jolts along at a moderate pace.

A driver and a guard sit on top. Banks of ominous thunderclouds
hover overhead.

INT. STAGE COACH - CONTINUOUS

Elizabeth is pressed into the corner of the seat beside a pudgy,
overdressed HUSSY. A GAMBLER sits across from them, taking an
occasional nip from a flask.

Elizabeth stares out the window.

INT. COACH - DAY

Elizabeth is asleep, wedged into the corner. The sky is black with storm clouds outside the window.

CRACK!

Elizabeth sits bolt upright. It could be thunder.

But the gambler pulls a small derringer from his boot. The hussy tugs her rings off her fat fingers and shoves them between her breasts as the stage rolls to a halt.

                         HUSSY
          Goddamn robbers!

Elizabeth gropes at her neck for the cross that isn't there. Her hand falls away.

                    DRIVER'S VOICE (O.S.)
          We ain't got no payroll!

Another shot CRACKS. A THUMP is followed by a chunk of wood flying by the gambler's window.

                    DRIVER'S VOICE
          My hands is in the air! Ain't nothing on this
          stage worth shooting me over!

                    GUARD'S VOICE
          You got the wrong stage, mister. Star Line went
          through yesterday!

Elizabeth cranes her neck.

Through her window we see the strongbox hit the dirt and a horse's hooves prancing in front of the stage.

A rifle barrel is aimed at the coach from a boulder twenty feet above the road.

                    COULTER'S VOICE
          If this is the stage to Albuquerque, I've got the
          right stage.

Elizabeth grabs the door handle and yanks it open.

                    COULTER'S VOICE
          Everybody out! Steady - no fast moves - or my
          partner and I will shoot to kill!

The hussy falls back against the seat, moaning. Elizabeth half-climbs, half-falls from the stage.

EXT. STAGE COACH - DAY

Clinging to the door, she sees Coulter on horseback. A second horse is tied a short distance away.

The wind whips Elizabeth's skirts as her gaze meets and locks with Coulter's - his accusing, hers pleading for understanding, for forgiveness.

The gambler joins her, grabbing her elbow.

                    GAMBLER
          Leave the ladies alone, you son-of-a-bitch. Take
          what you're after and get the hell out of here!

                    COULTER
          Drop your weapons and spill your ammunition.

The guard and driver break their weapons open and empty the shells into the dirt, then toss their guns.

                    COULTER
          You too, mister. Don't make me shoot you.

Elizabeth jerks her elbow free from the gambler.

The gambler smirks, raises his hands.

                    GAMBLER
          No guns, mister. I travel light.

Elizabeth whirls around. The hussy has the gambler's derringer. She aims through the window and cocks it.

Elizabeth springs toward the stage and slams the woman's hand against the side of the coach.

                    ELIZABETH
          You fool! He doesn't want your jewels!

Elizabeth twists her hand, the gun fires - BANG! - and falls to the ground.

                    HUSSY
          Goddamn you!

                    ELIZABETH
          Don't shoot!

She scrambles for the gun... snatches it up... whirls
desperately... grips it tightly in front of her - sweeping it back
and forth to cover everyone.

                    ELIZABETH
          Everybody! Just stop it!

She glares over her shoulder at Coulter.

                    ELIZABETH
          Are you crazy? Why did you follow me?

                    COULTER
          You left me.

                    ELIZABETH
          To protect you!

                    COULTER
          That makes a hell of a lot of sense!

                    ELIZABETH
          And you think this does?

                    COULTER
          Are you coming with me or not?

A fork of lightning splits the air - thunder CRASHES.

His horse rears, his front hooves flailing the air. Coulter
controls him with one hand on the reins, the other still aiming
the pistol.

                    COULTER
          I haven't got all day!

                    ELIZABETH
          You're crazy!

She starts toward him... the wind catches her bonnet and snatches
it from her head. He reaches for her - then pulls back, scowling,
his gun still trained on the others. Crazily... wildly... she
begins to laugh.

                    ELIZABETH
          How did you find me?

                    COULTER
          I've been following all day, until I could cut
          ahead to find a place to set up.

She glances up at the boulders above them.

                    ELIZABETH
         Is that Lucius up there?

Finally, a smile quirks the corner of his mouth.

                    COULTER
                   (sotto voce)
         Nobody. Just a straight stick. Now let's get the
         hell out of here.

Elizabeth turns back and stops... stares... at the strong box in
the road.

She starts for it, hesitantly at first, then with determination.

                    COULTER
         What are you doing?

She tries to lift it but it's too heavy.

                    COULTER
         Lady!

She aims the derringer and SHOOTS the lock off the box.

The hussy SCREAMS.

                    COULTER
         I said leave that damn thing here! I didn't come
         here to rob the stage!

Elizabeth flings the lid open and rifles through the contents. She
pulls out a several gold coins.

                    ELIZABETH
         We're not robbing it.

She hoists herself onto her mare ... tosses her head and flashes a
defiant smile.

                    ELIZABETH
         We're borrowing it.

                    COULTER
         If you don't drop that money I'll shoot you myself!

                    ELIZABETH
         I have my reasons.

Elizabeth fumbles in the purse dangling from her wrist and pulls
out her calling cards.

She rides closer to the stage.

                    COULTER
          Damnit lady!

Coulter trains his gun at the guard's chest.

                    COULTER
          Touch her and I'll kill you.

She holds several cards out to the guard. The man cringes back,
his hands held high. She flings the cards at him. The wind whips
most of them away but one lands at the driver's feet. He reaches
for it, fearfully.

                    ELIZABETH
          Consider this my I.O.U. I can assure you, you'll
          get the money back, every cent.

The driver reads the formal calling card:

INSERT:

CALLING CARD which reads: "Mrs. Elizabeth Cooke Dougherty"

BACK TO SCENE

                    DRIVER
          I - I heard about you! You're the one who was
          kidnapped by Boone Coulter! But that means -

Eyes bulging, he gapes past her at Coulter.

                    DRIVER
          Sweet Jesus!

The gambler and hussy press back against the stage. The driver and
guard thrust their hands higher.

Elizabeth pins the driver with a determined gaze.

                    ELIZABETH
          You can tell the authorities that my husband - the
          sheriff of Redemption, Texas is a liar and a
          murderer. I wasn't kidnapped. I ran away! I
          released Boone Coulter from my husband's jail. And
          I'm staying with him!

She kicks her heels into the mare's flanks and races up the
mountain.

A BOLT OF LIGHTNING AND a CRASH OF DEAFENING THUNDER scare the horse, but she kicks again, driving on.

She throws a glance behind her. Coulter is closing the distance between them.

The rain splashes down on Elizabeth as she throws her head back with an expression of jubilation.

INT. EL PASO SALOON - DAY

Winston sits alone in a noisy saloon, watching the door. He checks his pocket watch and sighs. But when he rises to leave, he is stopped.

Dougherty is standing behind him, clutching a bottle. Winston sinks back to his chair and holds up a folded paper as Dougherty takes a seat.

> WINSTON
> I thought you weren't coming, which would hardly be polite since you extended the invitation.

> DOUGHERTY
> Save your airs for that trashy little thing you've been hauling all over West Texas. I'm here for business.

Winston's lip curls as if he smells something rank. He probably does.

> WINSTON
> I don't know you, sir. I can't imagine what business we'd have together.

> DOUGHERTY
> That newspaper article you wrote. Why are you nosing around Boone Coulter's story?

At that, Winston smiles, points to his nose.

> WINSTON
> How apropos an analogy, sir. A reporter's nose often leads him where logic wouldn't, and quite successfully.

> DOUGHERTY
> Sometimes dangerously.

> WINSTON
> Is that a warning?

                         DOUGHERTY
          I want to know what you've found out about Coulter.
          Maybe we can help each other.

Dougherty slides some money across the table. Winston merely
pushes the money back to him.

                         WINSTON
          There's nothing to find out about him. Nobody knows
          a thing about him - except who he's killed.
          However, they all have one thing in common.

Winston watches the sheriff closely.

                         WINSTON
          They're all from Missouri.

Dougherty's grip tightens on the bottle.

                         DOUGHERTY
          A lot of people are from Missouri.

                         WINSTON
          From the same town? I wish I could help you,
          Sheriff. Your wife's situation must be difficult
          for you.

A cold smile further misshapes Dougherty's scarred features.

                         DOUGHERTY
          I'm not sheriff any more.

Dougherty pulls a folded, heavy paper from inside his coat and
tosses it to the table in front of Winston.

                         DOUGHERTY
          If she's still alive I'll catch her.

Curiosity and suspicion flicker in Winston's eyes.

                         WINSTON
          Catch?

He opens the poster. We don't see it.

                         DOUGHERTY
          Before long there won't be a crossroads in the
          southwest that doesn't have her likeness nailed to
          a post. I'll catch them, all right.

                         WINSTON
          Then you really don't need me at all, do you?

Winston rises, tips his hat.

> DOUGHERTY
> Let me tell you something, you arrogant son-of-a-
> bitch. You can clean up a whore, you can wash off
> the stink - but a whore's always a whore.

> WINSTON
> Funny. I thought we were discussing your wife. Good
> day, sir.

Dougherty leaps to his feet, yanks Winston to him.

> WINSTON
> I - I beg your pardon, sir. I'm not usually so
> insensitive.

Dougherty releases him slowly, then spreads his hand over the
wanted poster and crushes it.

> DOUGHERTY
> They're all alike.

EXT. MOUNTAIN TRAIL - LATE DAY

Coulter and Elizabeth are on a narrow, rain-slicked rocky trail.
Their horses are secured to piñon trees. The cliff below them
plunges hundreds of feet. The trail narrows to a ledge that curls
around the face of the mountain.

> COULTER
> There's a cave up ahead. It'll be safe for one
> night.

She starts to lift her carpet bag, but he yanks it away from her.
Startled, she draws back.

He opens it, rummages through it fiercely - pulls out the bottle
of laudanum. She manages not to look sheepish. Barely.

Without a word, he gives it a vicious hurl off the ledge of the
mountain, and it's swallowed up by the distance as it falls.

> ELIZABETH
> We might have needed that.

But one look from him, and she shuts up.

Coulter heaves the saddlebags to his shoulder and grabs
Elizabeth's elbow, pushing her toward the narrow ledge.

                        ELIZABETH
I can't.

                        COULTER
I don't care if you're scared. You got us into this
mess.

                        ELIZABETH
As if the whole world wasn't already chasing you!

                        COULTER
I didn't have much in this world, And you're fast
taking it away from me, every bit of it! I told
you I don't steal!

                        ELIZABETH
But you didn't steal, I did!

                        COULTER
We were together, damn you!

Elizabeth's response is quiet, triumphant.

                        ELIZABETH
    Yes. And now, because of what I did, we always will
    be.

Stunned, he releases her. She proceeds out on the ledge, where she
flings the gold coins over the edge.

INT. MOUNTAIN CAVE - DAY

Elizabeth faces Coulter; behind him the cave yawns dark. His
anger, his frustration with her is evident in his expression, the
tension in his body.

                        ELIZABETH
    We could go back to the cabin until they stop
    looking. Nobody will expect us to go back to Texas.

                        COULTER
    They won't stop looking this time.

He takes her by the shoulders and turns her, forcing her to look
out. A magnificent vista of canyon spreads below, and the sunset
sky is explosive with rolling clouds. There is an overwhelming
sense of height, of distance from the world. The wind HOWLS,
buffets the mountain.

Elizabeth closes her eyes and leans back against Coulter's chest.

                    ELIZABETH
    I know it must not seem that way ...I have never
    been an impetuous woman. The way you've known me,
    the things I've done ...
                    (shakes her head hard)
    It was never my intention to hurt you, to bring
    harm to you.
                    (beat)
    I should never have forced you to bring me.

He stiffens. His voice is cold.

                    COULTER
    And you're sorry you came with me.

                    ELIZABETH
    No! Never that!

He jerks away from her.

                    COULTER
    Don't lie to me!

                    ELIZABETH
                    (softly)
    I'm not lying.

                    COULTER
    Then you're a fool.

                    ELIZABETH
    Perhaps.

                    COULTER
    It's a hell of life for a lady.

                    ELIZABETH
    It's a hell of a life for anyone, Mr. Coulter. Are
    you going to tell me it's what you want?

                    COULTER
    You didn't know what you were choosing.

                    ELIZABETH
    And neither did seventeen-year-old John Wesley
    Bridges, when he killed his first man.

She reaches out to touch him.

                    ELIZABETH
    I love you, you know.

He freezes.

                    COULTER
        You can't. You don't know what you're saying.

                    ELIZABETH
        Don't tell me I can't! I do, and you can't change
        that. You can hurt me. You can put me through
        hell, but you can't stop me from loving you.

                    COULTER
        Don't preach at me!

                    ELIZABETH
        Then don't tell me not to love you! It's all I have
        left.

He jerks away from her, every movement crisp with tension.

                    COULTER
        I feel sorry for you, lady. That ain't much.

He yanks kindling from a saddle bag, begins building a small fire.

She tosses a stray stick at the pile.

                    ELIZABETH
        It's more than I had before.

EXT. HILL ABOVE LINCOLN, NEW MEXICO TERRITORY - DAY

High noon, and Elizabeth and Coulter rein in atop the last steep
hill overlooking Lincoln. The deserted road twists through the
settlement, lined by a dozen or so flat-roofed adobe buildings.
Only two buildings are taller: The two-story building that serves
as a courthouse and jail, and taller still, El Torreón, an old
adobe Indian watchtower.

                    ELIZABETH
        Are you sure it's safe?

                    COULTER
        Pat Garrett's still in Albuquerque, trying to claim
        his reward.

                    ELIZABETH
        It seems like a lifetime ago that I heard they'd
        killed Billy the Kid.

                    COULTER
        If people had any idea how hard it is to get the
        government to fork over a reward, they'd think

twice about going after a bounty.

She darts an uneasy look in his direction.

                    COULTER
          I'm going to get you out of this, Elizabeth. One
          way or another.

She turns her anguished face away from him.

EXT. LINCOLN - DAY

They approach the courthouse slowly. A small Mexican BOY Plays in the road.

Drawing near the building, Coulter swings off his horse.

                    COULTER
          Cover your head and wait here.

His spurs clink dully against the wood steps as he mounts them slowly. He's about to enter the door when he stops dead.

A tattered assortment of wanted posters are posted on the wall beside the door. One stands out: New, bold, clear. Instead of a crude line drawing, this one bears a photograph ... Elizabeth's wedding picture, accurately drawn.

It reads: "KIDNAPPED, Elizabeth Cooke Dougherty, $5,000.00 Reward, payable by Mr. Clayton Dougherty upon her safe return, Redemption, Presidio County, Texas."

Across the top of the poster is handscrawled: "WANTED FOR STAGE ROBBERY." The word "KIDNAPPED" and the phrase "upon her safe return," have been crossed through.

He turns quickly to her.

                    COULTER
          Susannah.

She frowns, confused.

                    COULTER
          Susannah. There's no need for you to come in. Wait
          for me here.

She looks over his shoulder and sees the poster.

                    ELIZABETH
          My God.

INT. COURTHOUSE - DAY

Three men play poker around a desk while a third STOOP-SHOULDERED MAN whittles a piece of wood. All faces turn toward Coulter as he enters; two reach for their holsters.

Coulter removes his hat and nods.

                    COULTER
          Afternoon. My wife and I are headed up toward
          Albuquerque, and we got wind there was a gang
          workin' this road. With no Marshall around, she's
          pretty scared.

                    CARD PLAYER #1
          Ain't no gangs working any roads round here. But if
          you're really worried, a stage'll be through in two
          days.

                    COULTER
          Can't afford a stage.

Coulter stares the man straight in the eye.

                    COULTER
          Besides. From the sound of things, the stages
          around here haven't been too safe.

The stoop-shouldered man squints up at him, jerks his chin toward the window.

                    STOOP_-SHOULDERED MAN
          You talkin' bout the poster outside? Y'ain't got
          nothin' to worry about from La Desperada.

                    COULTER
          La Desperada?

                    STOOP-SHOULDERED MAN
          That's what Harper's Weekly is calling her. That
          lady running with Boone Coulter. They aren't
          around here any more. They already held up another
          stage, right up near Cimarron.

Coulter's calm facade doesn't reveal a thing.

                    COULTER
          Cimarron? When?

                        CARD PLAYER #1
        A couple of days ago. Sheeyit! These cards ain't
        worth buffalo dung today.

He smiles genially, revealing rotten teeth.

                        CARD PLAYER #1
        Tell your little wifey she don't need to worry bout
        that lady outlaw and scum she's traveling with.
        They know better than to show up in Pat Garrett's
        territory.

                        COULTER
        I'll be sure to tell her.
                            (beat)
        Where's the Western Union office?

EXT. LINCOLN STREET - CONTINUOUS

Coulter mounts his horse and they ride down the street. Elizabeth
studies him, worried and surprised when he stops at the hotel. He
doesn't meet her eyes. He enters the hotel where a WESTERN UNION
sign is hung in the window.

A few moments later, he exits the hotel and strokes the mare's
nose before mounting. Elizabeth's hands are clenched tight on the
reins.

He heads out of town, Elizabeth following.

The small Mexican boy suddenly jumps in front of them and points
his finger.

                        BOY
        Pow!

EXT. ROAD - DAY

With the town out of sight behind them, Coulter finally stops and
lets Elizabeth catch up to him. He bites back a smile.

                        COULTER
        Do you know what we've done?

                        ELIZABETH
        Dear God, what now?

                        COULTER
        We've held up another stage. In Cimarron. Two days
        ago.

                              ELIZABETH
Now I know you're quite mad. Cimarron is two
hundred miles from here!

                              COULTER
I know that. You know that. But the people in
Cimarron know we robbed their stage.

                              ELIZABETH
That's preposterous. Why, I would never do such a
thing!

                              COULTER
There's no sense in ruffling up like a wet hen. You
did do such a thing, so you may as well realize
you'll be accused of more.

                              ELIZABETH
But we didn't! We wouldn't! Why, they'll be
accusing us of every holdup from San Antonio to
Laramie, Wyoming -

She smiles.

                              ELIZABETH
And that means they don't know where we are.

                              COULTER
     For now.

He clucks to his horse and rides on. Elizabeth catches up quickly
and rides beside him.

                              ELIZABETH
What were you doing at the hotel?

                              COULTER
Sending a telegram.

                              ELIZABETH
     To whom?

He's purposefully avoiding her stare.

                              COULTER
Your husband.

                              ELIZABETH
     What?!

                              COULTER
Don't worry. I'll have you safe on a stage to San

Francisco before I meet up with him.

                    ELIZABETH
What are you talking about? Meet up with him?

                    COULTER
I'm choosing my own ground, that's all.

                    ELIZABETH
But - but how do you think a telegram could reach
him? He could be anywhere!

                    COULTER
Everybody's going to be searching between Cimarron
and Seven Rivers, now. I sent a wire that only
Clayton Dougherty will understand.

EXT. CIMARRON HOTEL - DAY

Micah and Dougherty dismount before a two-story stucco building
with a courtyard/patio at the side, lovely flowers spilling from
terracotta urns. A hanging sign reads CIMARRON HOTEL.

INT. CIMARRON HOTEL - DAY

Cool and dark. Dougherty stands at the counter, signing in.

The clerk turns the book around and reading the name, hands
Dougherty a key.

                    CLERK
          Upstairs and to the left, Mr.
          Dougherty. Wait -

He calls back to the Western Union window -

                    __CLERK
          Who's that telegram for, that one that came in
          yesterday?

INT. WESTERN UNION WINDOW - DAY

An array of messages are pinned haphazardly to the bare wood wall
above him. The western Union Clerk yanks one down.

                    WESTERN UNION CLERK
          Sheriff Clayton Dougherty, Redemption, Texas..?
          Hell's bell's. I'm glad somebody showed up for it.

He shrugs and shoves it through the window.

Dougherty reads it, and frowns. Micah watches curiously from across the lobby.

                    WESTERN UNION CLERK
          Will there be a response?

                    DOUGHERTY
          None that you can deliver.

EXT. CIMARRON HOTEL - DAY

Dougherty scowls into the distance as Micah reads:

INSERT - CLOSE ON TELEGRAM

which reads "JOHN WESLEY BRIDGES WAITING IN LINCOLN"

BACK TO SCENE

                    DOUGHERTY
          So it ends in Lincoln. This is why I brought you,
          son. I need somebody I can trust.

Micah looks up, perplexed.

                    MICAH
          My name is Bridges.

                    DOUGHERTY
          I think we'd better have a talk.

EXT. STREAM THROUGH MOUNTAIN VALLEY - DAY

Elizabeth kneels near the fire where an enamel coffee pot is
heating on a flat rock.

She opens the small tin of henna, its paint flaking and edges
beginning to rust. A sprinkle of greenish powder sprays across the
back of her hand. She sniffs it, wrinkles her nose, rubs her
fingers across it and watches in horror as her skin turns orange.

                    ELIZABETH
          Oh, God.

She pours the henna into the coffee pot and stirs it with a stick,
making a face at the smell. Then she bends over the flowing
stream and starts pouring the mixture onto her hair, kneading the
muddy substance through.

EXT. SAME - DAY

Coulter rides along the stream, a young pronghorn antelope carcass
flung over his horse.

The campsite seems empty until Elizabeth emerges hesitantly from behind a bush. Her face is pale beneath a fiery halo of hair.

                    COULTER
     What the hell?

                    ELIZABETH
                    (bravely)
     I don't believe anyone will recognize me from the
     wanted poster now, do you?

He doesn't answer.

                    ELIZABETH
     It's ... bright, isn't it?

He nods mutely, still frozen to the saddle. Slowly, he begins to laugh.

                    ELIZABETH
     Mr. Coulter!

Sliding from his horse, he lets the antelope and rifle drop to the ground. He laughs until his legs give way, and he sits right there on the ground, still laughing.

Elizabeth balls her orange fists on her hips, waffling between tears and rage. Rage wins.

                    ELIZABETH
     It's not funny! It's not one damn bit funny. I did
     this to save your skin!

He can only shake his head and laugh harder. She grabs his shoulders, shakes him until he grabs her in self defense.

                    COULTER
     You're an amazing woman. You finally did it. You
     busted the hell out of that jar.

                    ELIZABETH
     The posters said I had yellow hair. You don't have
     to get rid of me, now.

He doesn't answer. She stays very still, her hands on his shoulders, her eyes blazing.

                    ELIZABETH
     Some things never change, do they?

                    COULTER
     If that's what you call me putting you on a stage

to San Francisco
- no, nothing's changed.

She flinches away from him.

He lifts a fist full of her hair. It spills through his fingers
like liquid fire, gleaming in the sunlight. He traces her face
with a callused thumb, stroking the fine red dye-line around her
temples. He tilts her face up to his, and -

She's beautiful.

                    ELIZABETH
          You warned me, didn't you? You said you'd make no
          pretty promises.

She tears her gaze away from his.

                    ELIZABETH
          Well, that's that. I won't be forcing myself on
          you. Not again.

                    COULTER
          You're talking foolishness.

                    ELIZABETH
          Am I? I gave you my life when you didn't want it. I
          held you at gunpoint and trusted you with it. And
          then, then I had to force my love upon you ...

                    COULTER
          Don't say that.

                    ELIZABETH
          Because you truly don't act as if you want it.

                    COULTER
          Don't ever say that.

He folds her against him, buries his face in her hair as she
clings to him.

                    COULTER
          You can stay. You have my word.

EXT. SEVEN RIVERS - DAY

Micah rides past the hotel where Winston is tipping his hat to a
sedate young woman on the steps.

                    WINSTON
     I'll return post haste, my dear.

                  YOUNG WOMAN
     I miss you already, sweetie.

At the sound of her voice, Micah snaps his head around to look.

He watches Winston trot down the last several steps and walk away.
The "sedate young woman" is none other than Doralee, all spruced
up. She enters the hotel.

INT. CIMARRON HOTEL LOBBY

Micah bounds up to the maid sweeping the floor.

                  MICAH
     Is there a Yankee dandy staying here?

                  MAID
     Oh, yes. Mr. Winston, the newspaper man. He's got
     the best room in the hotel, number 10.

                  MICAH
     Is he ... is he alone?

                  MAID
     He has a ... female companion.

Micah charges inside toward the stairs.

                  MAID
     Wait! You can't -

Micah jabs his thumb at his badge without slowing down.

                  MICAH
     Official business.

She gapes after him.

INT. HOTEL ROOM

Doralee is sprawled across the bed, half asleep. At the KNOCK on
the door she rolls over, turning her back to it. Another KNOCK.
Finally she pulls on a pretty wrapper and is tying the bow at the
waist when she responds.

                  DORALEE
     Come in.

The door squeaks open but nobody enters. She raises her face and her mouth falls open when she sees Micah.

                    DORALEE
    Where on earth did you come from?

                    MICAH
    I need to talk to you.

She hurries past him to close the door.

                    DORALEE
    Did anybody see you come in here? Lord, if Oliver
    comes back and catches you here, I'll never get to
    New York!

                    MICAH
    What are you doing here?

                    DORALEE
    He came, looking for Boone Coulter and Miz
    Dougherty. We're waiting on a wire from Missouri.

                    MICAH
    Missouri?

                    DORALEE
                (defensively)
    I told him the sheriff came out of Boone Creek, and
    he thought he'd check up on it. Nothing wrong with
    that.

But Micah hardly seems to be listening. He can't tear his eyes
away from her face.

                    MICAH
    I can't tell you how glad it makes me feel to see
    you.

                    DORALEE
    What are you doing here - where are you going?

                    MICAH
    To Lincoln. Don't ask me why, cause I don't know.
    But we're going to Lincoln. And I wouldn't let the
    sheriff see you. He hasn't been too happy about
    the things Winston is writing.

Doralee snorts.

                    DORALEE
    Who the hell cares what he thinks?

MICAH

Back in Redemption you made me the sweetest offer I
can imagine, and I've never forgotten it, and I've
never forgotten how awful I treated you.

She's embarrassed.

DORALEE

I don't want to talk about it. It was just
foolishness, that's all.

He sits down in a chair. She perches on the edge of the bed,
facing him. He fumbles with his hat between his widespread knees,
fighting for words.

MICAH

You always did think I was a fool, for honoring the
sheriff the way I did, didn't you?

DORALEE

Yeah, I guess I did.

MICAH

I don't blame you for that. It's just that he was
the one who - who saved me, he brought me out of
the place my mamma was at and saved me, and -

He catches his breath on a choked sob. Doralee, unable to stop
herself, moves to cradle his head against her bosom.

DORALEE

If you don't stop blitherin, like a dern fool ...

She sniffs loudly, wipes her face with the back of her hand.

DORALEE

I'm gonna slap the shit outta you.

She pulls her robe tight around her shoulders and shivers.

DORALEE

Look, Micah. I shouldn't tell you anything. I seen
stuff in Redemption I never told, that's for damn
sure. And I could've gotten Miz Dougherty in a lot
more trouble, a lot faster. But - well, Oliver is
finding out things. Things about the sheriff that
you aren't gonna like. I don't want to see you
hurt, but Micah, things are lookin' real bad.

MICAH

I reckon I know it. He does, too. He's actin'
strange. But I can't leave him. I owe him too much.

He stands up beside her.

                    MICAH
        Doralee ... I've been thinking on this for a long
        time. And there's something I want to do, if
        you'll let me. You shouldn't, but I sure hope you
        do. It's what I should have done that night, but I
        was too big a horse's ass.

She figures she knows what he wants. She looks sad, looks away,
finally shrugs.

                    DORALEE
        Sure. Why not?

Micah raises her chin with his finger and gives her the sweetest
kiss in the history of the world. And then, with Doralee too
stunned to move, he says--

                    _ MICAH
        I hope you make it to New York. You deserve that.

He is halfway out the door before she can react.

EXT. CAMPSITE BY THE STREAM

By flickering firelight we see a gun broken open, its chambers
empty.

Over the top of the gun Coulter's face comes into focus. He
reclines against his saddle. He has her book, holding it up to
read it in the firelight.

She snaps the gun shut.

He looks up, watches Elizabeth open the gun, snap it shut, each
time with more authority. Finally he reaches out and closes his
hand over hers.

                    COULTER
        Put it up. I don't like you fooling with that
        thing.

                    ELIZABETH
        It's not loaded.

                    COULTER
        You heard me. Put it up.

She eases her hand gently from his.

                    ELIZABETH
          I'm getting accustomed to it. I won't be caught
          unaware.

He springs across the space between them and starts to grab the
gun, but she holds it away, daring him. He finally lets his hands
rest on her shoulders.

                    COULTER
          I'm not going to let anyone catch you unaware. I'm
          not going to let anyone hurt you.

                    ELIZABETH
          Don't let them hurt you. That's all I ask.

He settles back against the saddle.

                    COULTER
          I found your poem.

                    ELIZABETH
          "What men or gods are these? what maidens loth?
          what mad pursuit?
          What struggle to escape?"

She stands and tilts her face up to the sky, spreading her arms
wide. A falling star streaks down and she catches her breath.

                    ELIZABETH
          "What wild ecstasy?"

Coulter stands, turns her into his arms. Right before he kisses
her --

                    COULTER
          I still think I'd stick to the Bible.

And as he kisses her, the Tears of St. Lawrence rain down
overhead.

                    ELIZABETH
          You can't convince me that you don't have poetry in
          your soul, Mr. Coulter.

She turns her face up to his, pleading.

                    ELIZABETH
          We don't have to go back to Lincoln. With Clayton
          expecting you to be there, it's the perfect time to
          get ahead.

                    COULTER
    I'm not running any more.

                    ELIZABETH
    Of course we're not running. We're just protecting
    ourselves the only way we can.

                    COULTER
    What did you think you were asking? That I would
    keep following your lead, keep running until I'm
    gunned down in the back like a coward?

She can't answer.

                    COULTER
    Say the word and I'll put you on that stage coach.

                    ELIZABETH
    I'll never say that word.

                    COULTER
    You're a damned stubborn woman.

She pulls away from him and breaks her gun open, and puts five
bullets into the chamber.

                    ELIZABETH
    Too stubborn to let you die alone.

EXT. MOUNTAINSIDE ABOVE LINCOLN - DAWN

Coulter enters the clearing. Elizabeth stares into the sunrise

                    ELIZABETH
    I've prayed he wouldn't get your message.

He watches her, wary.

                    ELIZABETH
    But - whatever happens, this is ours. They'll
    never take it away from us. And if this is all we
    have ... I do believe it's enough.

He joins her, not touching, staring at the rising sun.

Her eyes are resolute, refusing to see the future.

He sees the future, and can't bear it.

INT. WINSTON'S HOTEL ROOM IN LINCOLN - NIGHT

Doralee is alone in the adobe-walled hotel room. LOUD MUSIC and
LAUGHTER from the hotel dining room is muted in the background.

She turns to the rumpled bed and begins unbuttoning the jacket of
her demure gray suit. A KNOCK sounds at the door.

                    DORALEE
          All right, all right.

She yanks the door open with an exasperated sigh, to find Clayton
Dougherty filling the doorway.

                    DOUGHERTY
          Well, well, well ...

The amber light from the oil lamp illuminates his scarred face and
the large knife he holds so lovingly in his hand.

                    DOUGHERTY
          If it ain't our prissy-assed little whore.

He slings the door shut.

                    DORALEE
          Noo!

He slaps his hand across her mouth, cutting off her scream.

He grabs her hair, slams her head against the wall hard enough to
snap her cheekbone.

                    DOUGHERTY
          You gonna tell me what's going on here?

She tries to talk, but he rams her head against the wall again.

                    DOUGHERTY
          Why's that reporter sniffin' around?

Sobbing, moaning, she tries to nod her head. Anything. She'll do
anything, tell him anything, until - Wildeyed he gets in her face,
his hand dropping to her throat.

                    DOUGHERTY
          What did that little bastard Micah tell you? What
          did you tell him to turn him against me?

And even through the haze of pain, the blood, the tears, she
reacts to Micah's name. Her eyes narrow and harden in defiance as
she spits in his face.

EXT. WINSTON'S HOTEL ROOM IN LINCOLN - NIGHT

There is no one around to hear the MUFFLED SCREAM from within the room.

EXT. ROAD OUTSIDE LINCOLN - NIGHT

Elizabeth and Coulter approach the town on horseback. There is the distant sound of MUSIC and occasional RAISED VOICES.

The adobe tower, El Torreón, is unlighted but visible, silhouetted against the night sky.

Elizabeth's profile is gauzed and softened by moonlight, her hair covered by a shawl, as Coulter reaches across the open space between their horses and takes one of her hands, places something in her palm.

She unfolds the cloth wrapping and finds the coils of ribbon, the cross.

                    ELIZABETH
          It was never really mine.

                    COULTER
          It's yours.

She slips it over her head, tucks it into her blouse.

                    COULTER
          I'm going to check out a couple of places.

Elizabeth starts to protest, but he continues sharply.

                    COULTER
          One man alone is easy to ignore. If you walk into
          one of those places every eye will be on you. If
          Dougherty is there, red hair won't keep him from
          recognizing you.

                    ELIZABETH
          He'll recognize you!

                    COULTER
          If he sees me, he'll follow me out. He isn't going
          to do anything in front of witnesses. He's built a
          life on the illusion that he's an honest man. He
          sure as hell hasn't come this far to blow
          everything open.

                    ELIZABETH
          But --

                         COULTER
        I can take Dougherty in a fair fight and he knows
        it, so he won't fight fair. I need you to go to the
        top of the tower and cover me. You can see
        everything from up there.

                         ELIZABETH
        Don't you mean I'll be out of the way up there?

                         COULTER
        I need you, Elizabeth. For God's sake, don't argue
        with me over this.

After a strained silence, she nods mutely.

                         COULTER
        Cover me, but if anything goes wrong, promise
        you'll stay low, go back up into the mountains and
        stay there until it's safe. Dougherty's the only
        one who'd recognize you, and I guarantee, if I go
        down, he goes down with me.

She doesn't answer.

                         COULTER
        Promise me, Lady. Give me your word you'll stay
        safe.

                         ELIZABETH
        I can make that promise, but I can't promise that
        I'll honor it.

He squeezes his eyes shut.

                         COULTER
        Make it anyway.

                         ELIZABETH
                        (whispering))
        I promise.

INT. LINCOLN SALOON - NIGHT

Micah is alone at the bar, morose. Winston is across the room,
surrounded by eager listeners.

Winston breaks away from the crowd and comes up behind Micah.

                         WINSTON
        You've been nursing that same beer all night.

Micah doesn't answer, just scowls and stares straight ahead.

> WINSTON
> You've got it bad, don't you?

Again, Micah doesn't answer.

> WINSTON
> I imagine you'd take a swing at me if I told you
> you're better off without her, so I won't say it.

> MICAH
> She's better off without me, that's what counts.

> WINSTON
> What are you going to do when this is over?

> MICAH
> It's already over for me. I've done all I can. Now
> that you know all about Sheriff Dougherty ... Now
> that I know what he did to my mother ...

He breaks off, can't talk.

> WINSTON
> He isn't sheriff any longer. You are, Sheriff
> Bridges.

> MICAH
> I ain't no more sheriff than you are. Don't you
> know they probably elected another sheriff as soon
> as they got back to town?

> WINSTON
> Then don't go back.

> MICAH
> What?

> WINSTON
> Don't go back.

> MICAH
> I ain't got no place else to go.

> WINSTON
> Of course you do. Go forward.

Micah shoves off the stool, a little drunk.

> MICAH
> Take care of her, okay? I won't be here come

morning.

                    WINSTON
Tell her goodbye before you leave.

                    MICAH
Shit.

                    WINSTON
Whatever you've got to say, she'd rather hear it
from you.

EXT. RIVER - NIGHT

A light fog clings to the bushes, wafts through the low trees as
Dougherty kneels, washing his hands in the cold, flowing water.

He raises up, wipes off his knife blade, then looks back over his
shoulder toward the town, the loud MUSIC, and licks his lips. His
breath comes faster.

EXT. EL TORREÓN ROOF - NIGHT

The soft sound of RUSHING WATER from the nearby river blends with
NOISY SALOONS in the background as Elizabeth kneels, her hands
propped on the edge of the wall that encircles the flat roof of
the tower, clutching her pistol. A light mist clings to the air.
But the street below is visible.

Below, Coulter emerges from the shadow of the tower and crosses
the street, casting one last look toward her before entering the
first saloon.

Elizabeth shivers in the chill. She clutches the gun more tightly.

Moments later, he emerges from the saloon. She watches, restless,
breathless, as Coulter strides north to the next building, this
time without looking up at her.

Another shadow peels away from the saloon doorway, large and
hulking -

She cocks the gun and aims at the figure -

A woman. A large woman.

Elizabeth slumps against the wall, trembling, as Coulter passes
safely into the next saloon.

Moments pass. Longer. He reappears, alone. Her hands begin to
shake uncontrollably. As he enters the hotel, she slips the gun
into her pocket and clenches her hands to stop their shaking.

She leans against the low wall, pulling her shawl around her as a
couple stroll down the street below, the woman's laughter rising
and falling as the cowboy nuzzles her ear.

From below, Elizabeth's mare WHICKERS. She glances over her
shoulder anxiously at the noise, but the horse quiets. Turning
back to watch the hotel she rubs her hands together, reaches into
her pocket for the gun -

A hand slams over her mouth.

EXT. HOTEL - NIGHT

Coulter leaves the hotel, glances up at the tower. But between the
rising fog and darkness, he can't see much. He frowns uneasily,
then continues down to the White Elephant Saloon.

INT. WHITE ELEPHANT SALOON - NIGHT

Noise and smoke fill the air as Coulter makes his way to the bar.
He orders a drink and slouches over it, listening.

Across the room, most of the attention is focused on Winston who
is regaling the crowd with tales of faraway places.

                         WINSTON
          ... when I was in San Francisco with Emperor
          Norton. Now there's a strange man, a strange city,
          a strange tale ...

Coulter steps away from the bar as if to leave.

                      VOICE IN CROWD
          Never heard ol' Norton, and the Kid is dead - why
          don't you tell us about La Desperada? Now that's a
          story I wanta hear!

At that, Coulter eases against the bar and stays put.

EXT. EL TORREÓN ROOF

Elizabeth crashes against the low wall, her elbows striking the
edge, her eyes huge and wild as she struggles against her
attacker. She tries to scream, but the hand muffles her attempt
to a grunt.

Her attacker flips her over to her back and fastens his hand over
her throat, squeezing.

Choking she looks up into -

Clayton Dougherty's mocking, leering smile.

He pulls his hand away and she gulps, gasps at air, tries to cry out but her voice won't work.

                    DOUGHERTY
          Go ahead, Elizabeth. Scream.

She scrambles to her knees, lunges for the wall -

                    DOUGHERTY
          Bring him to me, Elizabeth.

She freezes. Below her, the street is foggy, empty.

                    DOUGHERTY
          It's your call.

                    ELIZABETH
          No.

                    DOUGHERTY
          Then you listen good and do what I say.

He wrenches her up, twists her arms behind her back until she arches in pain, but no sound escapes her. He tugs, and she can do nothing but what he wants. He forces her across the flat roof to the opening where the ladder waits.

                    DOUGHERTY
          I'm going to step down that ladder, and you're
          going to go with me, no funny business, do you
          hear?

                    ELIZABETH
          It's - it's not strong enough.

                    DOUGHERTY
          Then you'll die of a broken neck instead of a slit
          throat. What a pity.

Still gripping her wrists with one hand, he takes the first rung, then the second. She starts to kick, but he jerks her wrists and she bites her lip to keep from crying out.

                    DOUGHERTY
          You now.

She has no choice. She cooperates.

INT. WHITE ELEPHANT SALOON - NIGHT

Winston is surrounded by the crowd, relishing their attention.

                    WINSTON
          You'll have to wait for the next edition, folks.
          It'll send you into a swoon, I guarantee. I've got
          my sources. And my instincts. A good reporter
          follows his nose.

At the bar, Coulter slowly angles his face toward the crowd,
stares at Winston through narrowed eyes. Winston doesn't notice.

                    ANOTHER VOICE IN CROWD
          Mebbe you'd better blow your nose, mister, cause
          ain't nothing happening around here!

Loud laughter, back-slapping and guffaws fill the saloon as
Coulter, stone-faced, pushes away from the bar. Keeping his back
to Winston and the crowd, he weaves his way to the door.

EXT. WHITE ELEPHANT SALOON - NIGHT

Coulter steps into the street, staring straight ahead, manages to
walk several yards before finally raising just his eyes to the top
of El Torreón.

The moon and tower have been swallowed up by fog.

He glances around, then angles quickly for the tower.

EXT. RIVER - NIGHT

Dougherty circles Elizabeth, grazing her jaw, the nape of her
neck, her ear, with the tip of his knife. Finally he lets it rest
at her temple as she stands trembling, staring straight ahead,
refusing to react.

                    DOUGHERTY
          When I saw you and Coulter ride into town, I
          couldn't believe my eyes.

He digs the point into her temple and it begins to bleed. She
flinches, tries to wrench away, but he grabs her arm again, twists
it behind her until she sobs. He holds the knife to her throat.

But her other hand is free. She reaches for the folds of her
skirt, for the gun in her pocket --

                    DOUGHERTY
          What the hell is this?

He grabs a fist full of her hair and yanks her closer to him, spins her to face him --

                    DOUGHERTY
          What did you do to your hair?

He gives it an angry twist.

                    DOUGHERTY
          Parading around like you're better than everybody
          else, too good for Redemption --

                    ELIZABETH
          No, Clayton. Too good for you.

He backhands her. She staggers but remains standing, refuses to cry out. He grabs for her skirt, gathering it into his fist, hikes it up her legs. She fights, twists, tries to get to her gun, but it's bunched in the folds of her skirt.

He yanks her head, hard, and begins nicking her thighs with his knife.

                    DOUGHERTY
          Sing for me, Elizabeth. Let me hear you sing!

She fights it, bites her lip, but a vicious jab brings a moan. She muffles it with her hand, but his next jab brings a cry.

EXT. BASE OF EL TORREÓN

At the sound of Elizabeth's CRY Coulter sprints behind the buildings and runs along the river. Fog swirls, tendrils wrapping ghostly fingers around the trees, the bushes, as he breaks through the underbrush, gun drawn --

EXT. RIVER - NIGHT

-- and finds Dougherty standing over Elizabeth, his knife in his hand. He yanks her up and holds her in front of him, his knife at her throat, grinning.

                    DOUGHERTY
          That was real nice, Elizabeth. Real nice. I knew
          you could do it.

                    COULTER
          Let her go.

Dougherty slides his hand up her bloody thigh and squeezes.

                        DOUGHERTY
        Who you giving orders to? You talking to me?

                         COULTER
        This is between you and me, now. Let her go.

Dougherty laughs, a cold, hard sound.

                        DOUGHERTY
        I don't think so. She's between us now. Isn't she?

She tries to twist away from him. His knife breaks the skin at her
neck.

                         COULTER
        You coward.

                        DOUGHERTY
        Cowards live, haven't you learned that by now? And
        to the living go the spoils.

His voice roughens.

                        DOUGHERTY
        Hear that, Elizabeth? The spoils. That's you.
        Spoiled. Ruined. Dirty.

Coulter jerks his gun higher, aims -

                         COULTER
        I'm gonna make you pay for that--

                        DOUGHERTY
        Do it.

His knife bites into Elizabeth's neck.

                        DOUGHERTY
        You think you can shoot me without slitting her
        throat - do it.

Elizabeth gropes for the pistol in her pocket but can't get to it.
Each movement opens the fine, thin slice in the skin of her
throat. She finds the butt of the gun tangled in her skirt.

                        ELIZABETH
        No! Not for me! I'll not have you kill for me!

Coulter stands frozen. He can't shoot.

                        DOUGHERTY
        You should have known I'd get you back, Elizabeth.

I always keep what's mine.

                    ELIZABETH
          Not yours. I'm not yours!

She twists the gun in her skirts, turning it into Dougherty's side.

                    ELIZABETH
          I don't belong to anybody.

She pulls the trigger.

Dougherty's eyes widen and he convulses, slicing the side of her neck as he falls. She collapses to the ground beneath him.

Coulter lunges forward and, with one desperate heave, flings Dougherty's body aside and drops to his knees beside her limp, blood-soaked body.

                    COULTER
          No ... oh, God, no ...

Coulter reaches for the pulse at her neck and instead finds the bloody wound. Frantically he yanks the bandanna from his own neck and tries to bind it around her throat, fumbling with the knot - begging, pleading -

                    COULTER
          Lady, listen to me! You can't -- you can't die!

He pulls her limp body into his arms, rocking, clasping her against him like a child. Tears course down his cheeks.

                    COULTER
          Damnit, Elizabeth don't die on me.
          Don't give up don't -

His head falls forward over her body.

                    COULTER
          God - don't let her die. Please Jesus ... don't let
          her die.

EXT. RIVER - NIGHT

Micah bursts through the underbrush to find Coulter cradling Elizabeth's limp body in his arms.

EXT. LINCOLN - DAY

The morning is clear and bright as Coulter rides into town with a bundled body on a crude litter behind his horse. The mare follows on a long lead, riderless.

Head erect, skin drained, jaw clenched - he rides. As he makes his way down the winding road, faces appear in windows, people in doorways, silent, curious, gaping.

When he arrives in front of the courthouse, a small group of men are assembled, and in their midst, Micah Bridges, his badge gleaming. All eyes are on Coulter as he reins in, his right hand raised and his gun aimed skyward.

                    COULTER
     I'm Boone Coulter. I'm wanted in three states and
     two territories. I've killed seven men.
                    (beat)
     I'm turning myself in.

                    MAN IN CROWD
     It's a trick! He's lying!

Coulter trains his pain-dulled eyes on the man, silencing him.

                    COULTER
     This is Elizabeth Dougherty... Please give her a
     Christian burial and a stone fitting for a brave
     woman. A good woman. A ... a lady.

Coulter's face is lined with fatigue, etched with pain.

                    COULTER
     And on her stone, let it say, "Here lies one whose
     name was writ in tears."

A low MURMUR spreads through the crowd. Two pistols, one pearl-handled, one ebony, hit the dirt along with Coulter's rifle.

                    MAN IN CROWD
     How do we know he ain't lyin'?

Coulter slowly eases down from the stallion's back. Micah steps forward to the litter, swallows hard, as Coulter raises just the edge of the blanket covering her face.

Several people, the morbidly curious, strain forward to see. Micah swallows hard, blinks, finally turns his head away and nods.

                    MICAH
     I'm the sheriff of Redemption, Texas. And this --
     is her.

Coulter turns to Diablo and removes the saddle, the bridle. He slaps the horse's rump. It rears, flails the air with its hooves.

As Coulter watches the horse gallop away ...

                              COULTER
          It's over.

EXT. DORALEE'S LINCOLN HOTEL ROOM - NIGHT

A maid approaches with a covered tray of food, but Winston takes
it from her.

                              WINSTON
          Thank you, dear.

                               MAID
          That poor thing. I don't care what kind of girl
          she was, she didn't deserve what that monster did
          to her.

As the maid pads slowly away, Winston opens the door. Inside Micah
sits at the side of a bed, holding a woman's pale hand in his own,
his expression utterly bereft.

INT. DORALEE'S LINCOLN HOTEL ROOM - NIGHT

A lantern casts soft light and dark shadows across the bed where
we see the still, white body beneath the sheet, only one arm and
her head and shoulders showing ... and the mass of red hair
spilling across the pillow. She moans a raspy moan ....

Micah takes a small brown bottle labeled OPIUM. Carefully
squeezes ONE DROP into a teaspoon of water.

                              MICAH
          Come on. Just a little sip.

He attempts to spoon it between her lips. Her eyes open, mere
slits, and she whimpers, swallows, and winces in great pain.

Her throat is wrapped in white bandages.

She tries to raise her hand, but it falls limply to her side. She
sleeps.

INT. DORALEE'S LINCOLN HOTEL ROOM - NIGHT

Elizabeth's hair is plaited, but she is asleep. When she opens her
eyes, Winston is leaning over her bed. Startled, she begins to
raise up, but falls back on the pillows in pain.

                         WINSTON
          So ... at last we meet, Mrs. Dougherty.

Frightened, confused, she tries to draw away from him. Micah
speaks from the other side of the bed.

                         MICAH
          Miz Dougherty, I don't want you to strain yourself
          none, but Mr. Winston wanted to talk to you before
          he leaves tonight.

She reaches out her hand to Micah, her expression desperate, but
can only manage one word ...

                         ELIZABETH
          Coulter ...

Micah and Winston exchange glances.

                         WINSTON
          He's in jail, ma'am.

She squeezes her eyes shut, shakes her head, winces. Then
remembers.

                         ELIZABETH
          Clayton - did I kill him?

                         MICAH
          Yes ma'am.

                         ELIZABETH
          Good ...

She leans back against the pillow, drained, defeated.

                         MICAH
          Coulter turned himself in ... to save you. To stop
          the manhunt.

Tears roll down her cheeks, but she barely moves, can barely
speak.

                         ELIZABETH
          It wasn't supposed to end this way.

                         WINSTON
          I think the man has lived his whole life without a
          prayer of redemption. Perhaps this is the only way
          it could end for him.

Elizabeth turns her head away - and stares straight at the bottle of opium on the table beside her head. Catches her breath.

                         MICAH
          And Mr. Winston here helped, by - by claiming that
          you -

He breaks off, unable to speak.

                         WINSTON
          We had to explain somehow who you were. I was
          traveling with a ... a companion ... Well, I'm
          afraid that what we're trying to tell you -

                         MICAH
          You remember Doralee, ma'am. The sheriff killed
          her, the same night he tried to kill you. The
          doctor said it's a miracle you're alive.

                         WINSTON
          Elizabeth Dougherty is buried in a grave a mile
          down the road, ma'am. As far as the world is
          concerned, her run is over.

She finally pulls her gaze away from the opium.

                         ELIZABETH
          And I am ...

                         WINSTON
          A ... soiled dove, ma'am.

                         ELIZABETH
          You must be quite an adept liar, sir, if anyone
          would believe that.

Winston cocks his head toward her braid and arches his brows. She
touches it, and her eyes widen.

                         ELIZABETH
          Good lord.

                         WINSTON
          I am an accomplished liar, but you'd already
          provided some rather convincing evidence.

Elizabeth draws herself up, an incredible strain, but she is a
very determined lady.

                         ELIZABETH
          I want to see Mr. Coulter.

                         MICAH
He's at what used to be the Murphy Dolan Store, but
now they use it as a courthouse. They've got
Coulter upstairs. The governor's sending a whole
slew of guards down to fetch him. Pat Garrison's
recruiting them himself. There's no way you can --

                       ELIZABETH
When?

                         MICAH
In two days.
                       (a beat)
He gave me his - I guess, my family Bible. Did you
know my mamma named me after her daddy? A reverend?
Sometimes I get so confused I don't know who or
what to believe, any more. Who I am.

Elizabeth's eyes fill with tears and she takes his hand.

                       ELIZABETH
You're a fine man, Micah. Just listen to your
heart. It has never led you wrong.

She turns her head toward Winston, fixes him with a piercing
stare.

                       ELIZABETH
And when do you plan to expose my existence, Mr.
Winston?

                        WINSTON
Believe me, this is not easy for a newspaper man.
But it would serve me no purpose that I could live
with to expose you. It's over, ma'am.

                       ELIZABETH
Is it? Is it really?

She lies back against the pillows, closes her eyes.

                       ELIZABETH
I need sleep. I need to be alone.

The two men leave. They don't see her reach for the bottle of
opium with a trembling hand.

INT. LINCOLN COUNTY JAIL - NIGHT

The wind HOWLS outside. Coulter is crouched alone in the dark, his back pressed into the corner.

The sound of quiet FOOTSTEPS climb the stairs outside his door. A
RUSTLING noise of someone approaching. Keys RATTLE in the lock.
Slowly, the door creaks open.

He raises his eyes to a cloaked figure, to a gun trained on him.
The hood of the cloak falls back. Elizabeth. Pale as death in the
moonlight, her neck bandaged.

Coulter leaps to his feet, starts forward, stops and balls his
fists.

                    COULTER
          Elizabeth! How did you --

He casts a desperate glance over her shoulder.

                    COULTER
          You've got to get out of here! They'll hang you if-
          -

She stops him by placing her fingers over his mouth. He grabs her
hand, kisses it, pulls her to him. They cling together.

                    COULTER
          My God, my God, what are you doing here? This is
          crazy.

She pulls away from him and raises her chin, exposing her bandaged
neck. He winces.

                    ELIZABETH
          I'm here to release you. But only if you agree to
          my terms ....

                    COULTER
          What the hell are you talking about? What goddamn
          terms?

                    ELIZABETH
          I'm going with you.

                    COULTER
          Are you crazy? There are guards --
          the whole territory of New Mexico will be after us
          this time!

She stiffens and pulls away from him. There's no denying the fire
in her eyes, her voice.

                    ELIZABETH
          Either way, we go together. Is this where you want
          to die?

He can't answer.

                    ELIZABETH

          Then come with me.

She holds out her hand and he clutches it. He follows her through
the open door to the stairs.

INT. LINCOLN COUNTY JAIL - FIRST FLOOR - NIGHT

Elizabeth and Coulter emerge from the stairwell. Micah waits by
the door. Stunned, Coulter stares around the empty office.

                    COULTER
          What the hell is going on? Where are the guards?

                    MICAH
          Well, nobody thought it strange that I wanted to
          guard you, seein as how I'd already lost one reward
          off you. So while they was out on the porch
          playing cards, I took 'em some coffee ....

Micah motions to a closed door on the other side of the room.

                    MICAH
          They're tied up pretty good. They won't be raising
          a ruckus for quite a while.

                    COULTER

          Coffee?

                    MICAH
          It was Miz Dougherty's idea.

                    COULTER
          I'll just bet it was.

For a moment, neither speaks. Coulter gruffly offers his hand, and
Micah grabs it in a hard shake.

                    COULTER
          Live up to your name, son.

                              MICAH
        Yes sir.

Elizabeth grabs a mug of coffee from the desk.

                            ELIZABETH
        Here -- drink it!

                              MICAH
        Beggin' your pardon, ma'am, but if they're gonna
        blame me for being a fool again, at least this time
        I want some evidence that I was really bushwhacked.

He holds a pistol out to Coulter, wincing a bit.

                              MICAH
        Just put my lights out for a little while. I won't
        raise an alarm 'til daybreak, nohow.

Coulter snatches a rifle from the gunrack, his holster from the
desk, snaps at Elizabeth --

                             COULTER
        You thought of everything, did you?

Elizabeth bristles.

                            ELIZABETH
        Somebody had to.

Face to face, they glare at each other. Coulter gentles first.

                             COULTER
        We've got a long road ahead of us, Lady.

                            ELIZABETH
        I'm banking on that, Mr. Coulter. I'm banking on
        that.

EXT. A MOUNTAINSIDE ABOVE LINCOLN - NIGHT

Two riders, one in a billowing cloak, ride up the mountainside,
silhouetted against the rising moon.

Freeze.

                                              FADE TO BLACK.

PATRICIA BURROUGHS (POOKS) is a fifth-generation Texan who lives in Dallas with her husband, near her three sons and their families.

Her earliest memories are of long afternoons spent soaking up the drama and laughter of the silver screen, and of long nights absorbing the magic of the written word by flashlight. As a teenager, she sang, danced and acted in community theater productions.

These influences, she believes, are the foundation of her lifelong ambition to write, to spin the dreams that ignite imaginations—to repay the debt to those who reached through the klieg lights, flashlights and footlights to touch a young girl's heart.

She began her writing career with five published novels before being lured to the dark side, to screenwriting. After a career there that included uncredited but paying work, she returned to novels and is now writing a fantasy trilogy.

Find out more about Pooks—her books and other projects, and where she will be appearing at conferences, classes and readings—on her websites:

http://patriciaburroughs.com
http://planetpooks.com

Book View Café is a publisher and professional authors' cooperative offering DRM-free ebooks in multiple formats to readers around the world. With authors in a variety of genres including mystery, romance, fantasy, and science fiction, Book View Café has something for everyone.

Book View Café is good for readers because you can enjoy high-quality DRM-free ebooks from your favorite authors at a reasonable price.

Book View Café is good for writers because 95% of the profit goes directly to the book's author.

Book View Café authors include Nebula and Hugo Award winners, Philip K. Dick and Rita award winners, and *New York Times* bestsellers and notable book authors.

http://bookviewcafe.com